Cannibalia:

A Feast of Horror and Suspense

By: William Tull

CANNIBALIA: A FEAST OF HORROR AND SUSPENSE is an original publication. This work has never appeared in book form. The work is a fictional anthology, with all stories written and published entirely by the author. Any similarity to any actual persons, places or events is purely coincidental.

Text Copyright 2020 by William Tull

All illustration copyrights are granted to the specific artists of each piece created by them

ISBN: 9798647437273

All Rights Reserved, which include the right to reproduce this book or any portions thereof in any form whatsoever except as provided by the U.S. Copyright Law.

Edited by: Xeike Tull

For my wife, Xeike.

The love of my life.

My biggest fan and my harshest critic.

Table of Contents

Introduction

What you hold in your hands is the culmination of many months spent accumulating, writing, fretting, re-writing, hand wringing, editing, re-re-writing, and finally curating. Most of these stories were written on a whim, stories like "*Soft Serve*" and "*Battle of the Band*" started as a small idea and worked backwards to form a raucous romp of putrescent violence and humor. Others like "*Angel of Mercy*" started as vivid dreams that I couldn't get out of my head without putting on paper. Others had a direct purpose with intent to be used elsewhere. "*Little Stevie*", "*Redline*", "*Bloody Foot Prints*", and "*Vacant Eyes*" were all part of a larger project. Finally, the main course, "*Cannibalia*", was inspired by another horror anthology called "*Bon Appetit*" published by Infernal Ink Books.

Within "*Bon Appetit*", many writers I respect and publishers I've worked with put together a literary banquet of horror, all themed around cannibalism. As I read through the stories, both my appetite and my creative brain were hard at work, imagining an epicurean feast that would both fascinate and terrify.

In addition to these stories, you'll find original artwork from several of the most talented people I know. Each picture was created just for the story it is attached to. If the stories do not satisfy that primordial need that brought you here, the artwork surely will. Each picture has the artist name clearly attached with a full artist credit near the end of this book.

Without further ado, I present *"Cannibalia: A Feast of Horror and Suspense".* I hope you are as excited to read these stories as I am to share them with you.

"Little Stevie" by Colter Burkey

Little Stevie

I used to go to school with a kid named Steven Wilder. Everyone just called him “Little Stevie”, even though no one knew who “Big Stevie” might be. Little Stevie was a scary kid. The sort of kid that was always making problems. With his parents, the cops, at school - anyone, anytime, anywhere.

Stevie was ten. Old enough to be in fifth grade, but he got held back when he had to go to a boys’ home after starting some fires. He wasn't allowed to attend the regular class anymore after Mr. Muffins, the class hamster, was found impaled on a geometry compass. Instead, he went to the class with all of the special kids, but had to have his own special teacher assigned after he pushed a disabled boy off the slide for taking too long.

Stevie wasn't allowed to ride the bus but no one really knew why. One of the kids on the bus saw him one morning, kneeling over a dead dog that had been run over by a car. Stevie had a forked stick and was using it to spool the dog's intestines like spaghetti. The office staff had to call his mom to bring him a clean shirt when he got to school as his was smeared with blood and guts, making him smell like death.

Stevie's mother was a perpetually nervous lady, held hostage by his volatile temper. She always seemed like she was always scared of him and would do anything to keep him from having one of his screaming fits. When Stevie had a fit, he wouldn't stop until his throat went hoarse, and then he would start to kick and flail. He would bash his head on the ground or on the wall. The janitor tried to clean one blood stain off the wall in the cafeteria, but he only smeared it around and now it's just an orange smudge on the white drywall.

Stevie had a party for his sixth birthday. It was a get-together at a local park, and though Stevie had no actual friends, a few of us from school went. Everyone was having an okay time, playing the simple games and enjoying the park. Instead of a big cake, there were cupcakes being served. Stevie said he made them himself and he wanted everyone to try one, and we did. The people at the party were all enjoying their little pastries, until someone's mom noticed the chocolate chips were actually rat feces.

One day in his special class with his teacher, Mr. Larsen, Stevie was playing with Play-Doh. Little Stevie loved the Play-Doh best of all. He would twist up shapes, figures, scenery, and build little cities and matching people. He would spend all day on his projects and at the end of the day, took the most joy in smashing his creations. He would squeal in delight as each one was flattened and demolished under his clenched fists. Like Godzilla through downtown Tokyo.

On this day, Stevie was going above and beyond in his creation. All day long he toiled and created. He combined all of the colors he had available: yellow, orange, brown; and he sculpted a lion. He used white and black to put big friendly eyes on it and with his thumbs turned the lion's mouth up into a big friendly smile.

When class ended, Mr. Larsen complimented the project, it was so unlike anything Stevie had created before.

Stevie was so proud and so happy and for the first time ever, he asked Mr. Larsen to smash it.

Mr. Larsen wasn't sure if he wanted to, so detailed was the lion sculpture, but Stevie would not take "no" for an answer. He bounced up and down, squealing with delight as he urged Mr. Larsen on. It was only when Stevie started to grow frantic, his voice getting shrill, and his cheeks getting red, that Mr. Larsen relented.

He looked down at the smiling lion, its face framed by the lofty orange mane. He brought his hand up high. Stevie cheered him on, his little hands clutched about his chest.

Mr. Larsen brought his big hand down hard to annihilate the lion in one mighty blow!

Mr. Larsen screamed and cried out for help as a spray of blood spattered across Stevie's face. Mr. Larsen yanked his hand back and spun away from the table. He was clutching his wrist as blood ran freely from several open wounds on his hand. Embedded deep in his palm was one of the razor blades Little Stevie had hidden within his sculpture.

Stevie was still laughing when the ambulance arrived. After the incident, Mr. Larsen was gone for a long time. We never saw Little Stevie again.

Soft Serve

It all happened on a glorious summer day, the first nice day of the year. My friends and I had stopped at McDonalds after riding our bikes. It was a day made all the more wonderful by the fact the soft serve ice cream machine was actually working. None of my crew had money for ice cream, unfortunately, so we got our fountain sodas and sat to watch the crowd. We lamented this when we first arrived, but it soon became the luckiest thing that ever happened to us.

Chocolate and vanilla cones adorned the hands of every man, woman, and child who poured from the front doors, gleeful smiles all around. Milkshakes and McFlurrys galore, of every size and shape they could provide. The customary burgers and fries were soon forgotten in the tidal wave of frozen, sugared cream.

It was around noon when the vanilla started to flow forth with a slight pink tinge. Everyone must have assumed it was strawberry. None of the kids minded, but the adults said the flavor was off. Even still they continued eating it. A cold treat on a hot day was not going to be wasted. The chocolate was rich and dark, and as the afternoon waned, it only grew more intensely so.

The strawberry ice cream began to grow soft and syrupy, and the cones started to run and drip before they were even passed across the counter. The delicate spiraling shape began to grow muddy and far less appetizing, but a discounted price kept them moving freely into the hands, and mouths of the eager consumers. The taste was far less satisfying and many cones began to end up discarded by all but the most eager of them.

The line was still backed up to the door when the call went out that the machine had stopped working.

No one had expected it to work this long anyway and those turned away looked covetously upon those whose hands and cheeks were stained with the red syrup of their rapidly decaying cones. A smug sense of elitism went out through those who had the pleasure of snagging the last few cones. The early birds had caught their worms and the ones late to the party could only look on helplessly as the manager came out to open the machine and investigate the source of the disruption.

The gathered crowd fell silent when the manager, in her tight button down shirt, fell away from the machine, vomit cascading from her trembling lips. One of the teenagers who worked the deep fryer moved to take her place, and reached into the machine, probing around with a bare hand. He was visibly confused when he pulled out a long, milk-sodden clump of hair with a ragged, dripping chunk of scalp attached to it. There was clearly an ear dangling from the chunky flap of skin that swung from the tangled knot of hair. He clearly didn't recognize it for what it was, however, and casually dropped it to the tiled floor. The *splat* it made when it hit was like a gunshot to the gathered crowd.

People began to scream. Parents slapped the cones from their children's hands. Those in the front of the store began to heave and cough, projectile vomiting the warm and heavy contents of their stomachs onto the counter and the floor beyond. The chain reaction of nausea overtook those farther back and the sounds of violent retching and viscous fluid hitting the floor became a symphony of putrescence.

The exit became choked with bodies. All clawing and fighting their way out. All of them disgorging their gullets onto those in front of, and below, them. The shortest of them and the children got it the worst, of course. Each of them panicking with tears in their eyes and bile in their throats. They coated one another in their involuntary reverse of peristalsis.

The mass finally cleared and like a cork from a champagne bottle, they exploded free into the parking lot. Vomit stained the sidewalk, and in turn, the asphalt with that same even pink hue. Those who had been jogging towards the door in hopes of partaking in a sweet treat began sprinting away as the deluge of sweaty flesh and hot barf spilled free. Hot on their heels was an oily cloud of fetid stench that threatened to blacken the groomed hedges and drop birds from the sky.

Inside, still confused, the teenager at the machine fished another fleshy chunk out from the machine, his hand stained red up to the elbow. This time, as he withdrew a mangled hand from the reservoir at the top of the machine. The nails were cracked and split, and the fingers hung lazily, only barely connected to the splintered bones within. He recognized this for what it was and he fainted, falling flat on his back. The hand splattered to the floor next to him, displacing a small spot in the pink pool that was slowly spreading across the floor and creeping into the drain. Outside, the screams of the people in the parking lot were slowly over taken as the sounds of police and ambulance sirens grew near.

My friends and I were no longer sad we couldn't get ice cream. In fact, like many of the people who were there that day, we don't care much for it anymore.

The McDonalds was closed for a long time, and we never did find out who was in the machine or how they had gotten there. Everyone in town swears that when the weather turns nice, and the sun heats up the parking lot, you can still smell traces of that beautiful summer day.

"Bloody Footprints" by David Lipscomb

Bloody Footprints

When I was five, I found a dead body at the end of our driveway. I had gone down to check the mail, part of my morning chores, and there was a white station wagon stuck in the ditch. The front end was distorted and smeared with blood and hair. I remember seeing a few tangled strands blowing in the breeze. The body was that of a man, all twisted up and gray skin. His limbs were splayed unnaturally. I didn't know what

I was seeing. I thought he was going to move at any moment. There was so little blood that it seemed he was just resting or trying to play a joke on me.

His eyes never blinked, though. The red and purple mottling of his pale skin was clearly not normal.

I'm not sure how long I was there watching, but movement caught my eye. Someone had climbed out of the car, trying to sneak away without being seen.

She was older, not what I would call *old*, but her hair was the sort of blonde that would be white in a few years. She wasn't wearing any pants that I could see, instead she had a long brown T-shirt on and nothing on her feet. She was dressed like she was going to bed.

I remember thinking how strange it was to see her dressed like that. People didn't go outside like that.

She had a surreal look to her. Her hair was mashed up in a messy bun, and though she had make up on, it wasn't very good. It was as though she had put it on in the car in a hurry, or it was still on from the day before. The red on her lips was caked on thick. So thick it had stained her teeth and smeared up her cheeks, giving her large clown lips that made it impossible to tell where they really ended. As if to add to the derelict clown motif, she had bright blue eye shadow that was smearing into the eyeliner that was collectively running down her cheeks like black tears.

She crawled out from the driver's seat, and stopped when she saw me, staying hunched as she ducked behind the car.

She smiled, I think to disarm me, but her yellow teeth, smeared pink, scared me. My hesitance made her smile turn ugly and mean. Her lips turned up, and even through the smears of lipstick I could see the rot of severe gingivitis in her gums. The pink giving way to brown. Her gums receded so far that her teeth were long and spindly and seemed to dangle in her mouth. I was certain she was a vampire.

I was frozen. Even as she held her skinny fingers out towards me, beckoning me close, I remained stuck where I was. The fake nails on her fingers were blood red and cracked up the middle. There was a deep orange cigarette stain between her index and middle fingers. She smiled again and started towards me, her bare feet scraping the gravel in the ditch as she lurched forward. Then, just as suddenly, she stopped and shrank away to hide in the bushes nearby.

My mother scooped me up from behind and started to carry me back towards the house at a run. She was screaming for my father to call the police, call an ambulance, call anyone. Someone was hurt.

I peered up over my mother's shoulder, back at the scene of the accident. I could see the woman crouched near the car, slinking into the bushes, wild-eyed and smiling. We made eye contact and she held one of her fingers to her lips, pressing hard in a "Shh" motion.

The police came. An ambulance came. Even a fire truck came. I was stuck in the house though. I wasn't allowed outside and certainly not allowed to talk to anyone. Both my parents were at the end of the driveway. I could see them, though it was pretty far away. We had a very long driveway. As I watched them, imagining myself playing with the siren and the radio of the police car, something caught my eye.

The woman crawled out of the hedges close to my house. She was watching me in the window and as soon as I saw her, our eyes locked. She moved, hunched over across the gravel. She wasn't crawling, but more like a three point crouch, disjointed and pained in her movements. Her feet were filthy and bleeding. The gravel was sharp and there were lots of thorny brambles in the bushes along the driveway. She cast a slow look at the police, my parents, and everyone else at the end of the driveway. Then she slowly looked back to me, smiling that angry, exaggerated smile. I realized that now she was between me and any sense of safety I had.

Then she started towards the door.

She never rose; staying low like some sort of animal, but she hurried, leaving a trail of bloody foot prints in the gravel and then on the stairs leading up to the door. It was unnatural to see, all the more so as she kept her eyes fixed on me. I was numb, in throes of the overwhelming sense of panic that overtakes kids when they are truly frightened. Somehow, a primal sense of urgency overtook me and I ran to the door and locked the deadbolt seconds before she slammed against it from the outside. I fell back to the floor, either from the impact or from the sudden shock. I held my breath as the door knob rattled and the door shook, but the bolt held fast.

I saw her face in the window above the door as she stretched up to her extreme tip toes, the whites of her eyes huge and frantic as she looked in, leering down at me.

She made a scream like some sort of injured dog, almost like a yelp of anger and she started at the door again. I covered my ears, closed my eyes, and started to scream.

The sound stopped for just a moment, and I braved a look up, and just outside the window I had been watching my parents from, there she was. Her hot breath was fogging the window, her narrow shoulders heaving, and her hands now bleeding and smearing blood on the window as she ran her fingers down it and just… stared at me.

She turned suddenly. My screams having attracted my parents and an officer who were running back down the driveway.

She bolted back through the hedges and out the thick foliage beyond, and finally disappeared into the woods at the edge of our property.

My parents scrambled to unlock the door, bursting in when the deadbolt flipped over. My mother fell on me and cried, holding me tight and rocking until she, at least, felt better.

That night, I kept having nightmares that the woman had gotten into my house. I dreamt that I had woken and she was there at the foot of my bed, her eyes unnaturally huge and her mouth opening wide to swallow me up whole. I startled awake, alone in my room, but the echoes of her wild breathing seemed to linger in my ears.

The next day the police called to tell us they had found the woman. She suffered from dementia, and the man in the ditch was her husband who had been trying to take her to the hospital. They had a fight there on the side of the road and she had run him down with their car.

They found her at the neighbor's house. She had killed their small dog and was trying to get into the garage. My parents always told me how lucky we were that she never got into our house.

Never mind the bloody footprints that forever stained the rug at the foot of my bed.

Redline

Tyler and Tony were just outside of Bakersfield, in the sixth hour of an eight hour drive, bound for a music festival deep in the endless expanse of the Southern California desert. The sun had just gone down when they passed a young woman with her thumb out and a small bag over her shoulder. She was in a dusty leather jacket and hiking boots, and not much else. Her jean shorts were the last vestige of a pair of Levi's that was only barely enough to be considered clothing at all.

Her crop top was not much better. She had short cropped black hair and a pallid complexion that reflected the light of the head lights.

Tyler looked to his brother, who was looking to him. It had been a long drive, and they were late to get in the gate, but it hadn't been THAT long, and they weren't THAT late. There was the chance she was going to the festival, and after all, they were both young men out for a good time on a long weekend. Maybe she was looking for a good time over the long weekend too? Tyler slowed the car and pulled over.

She made short time catching up to them. In the time it had taken them to make a decision, Tyler was sure they had gone a quarter mile or more, and would have to back track. By the time he had stopped she was already jogging up behind them without so much as breaking a sweat. Tyler convinced himself that he had been driving too long, apparently, and his sense of time and distance were thrown off. Either that, or she was just a really fast runner.

She climbed into the back seat. The dome light bloomed above them, this let them get a better look at her, and allowed her a better look at them in kind. She was lovely, in that grungy punk rock sort of way, and both Tyler and Tony sat up straighter, smoothed their hair back and smiled. Tony angled the rear view mirror casually.

She introduced herself as Molly. Both the guys were very impressed with Molly's aesthetic, and were eager to get the ice breaking. Tony turned in his seat to face her, straining a little against his seat belt as Tyler pulled the car back onto the road.

"So where are you headed?" Tony asked, trying

to keep his tone cool.

"Let's turn up the music!" She replied, leaving thc question as though she hadn't heard it.

Tony was glad to oblige, turning up the music as they rocketed down the highway.

"Are you going to the festival?" Tyler called back to her.

"The what?" Molly called back, seeming distracted as she dug in her bag.

"Oh the music festival out here, EDM? You know? It's huge!" Tony said exuberantly.

Molly was still rifling around in her bag, but she angled her eyes up, clearly not knowing, and looked mildly annoyed at being pressed about it.

"Oh… yeah. Totally." She said, as though just remembering.

"No shit? Us too! We can take you all the way to the gate if you want. Are you camping out there? I can't believe Digital Diabolus came out of retirement for this show, right?!" Tony said, excited, as he tended to get when talking about his favorite artist.

"Oh…Yeah. Totally. Hey, can I smoke in here?" She asked, derailing the conversation as she pulled out a beaten pack of cigarettes from her bag.

"Sure!" Tony exclaimed.

Tyler shot his brother a withering look. There was no smoking allowed in the car, borrowed as it was from their parents. Tony responded with a shrug as Molly lit up. Tyler cracked the window, hoping the smell wouldn't linger.

As she smoked, Tony turned in the front seat to face her once again, going to strike up the conversation, despite the fact Molly looked agitated. Tony had never really been able to read women, and thought maybe that was just how her features rested. The puff of smoke she blew in his face was answer enough. He turned aside as he exhaled from his nose, a sneeze building up behind his eyes.

It was then he got a glimpse in her open bag. In the low light of the car stereo he saw clearly what appeared to be a human hand. The skin tone was a pallid blue, and the nails split and bloody. Molly reached down and jerked the flap closed on the bag and gave Tony a scathing look. She flicked her cigarette out the window, though it was hardly even half smoked.

Tyler was oblivious in the driver's seat, though even in the dark and with the music loud, Tony's gasp and pale complexion told him something wasn't right.

Molly licked her lips in the back seat, motioning to Tony as she leaned forward between the seats. Her demeanor had somehow… shifted. From tense and annoyed to sultry, almost lusty. Tony was unsettled, but there was something in that look. He swore her eyes flashed red when his own met hers and he leaned over as she whispered in his ear.

"I'm going to tear your fucking throat out..." She said with a husky whisper.

"What?" Tony asked, visibly confused.

Suddenly she was on him.

Tyler swerved as Tony started to thrash and yell.

Molly had latched her mouth onto Tony's neck, her teeth tearing right into his jugular. A red mist spewed forth across Molly's face and neck, across the windshield, and onto his brother.

"What the fuck!" Tyler yelled as he slammed on the brakes.

The car was in the middle of a swerve, and it caused the wheels to lock up. Tyler lost control of the car and they spun out as the wheels left the pavement and hit the loose dirt of the shoulder.

Time seemed to slow as Tyler fought against the wheel while Tony was screaming and lurching. Tony tried, at first, to dislodge himself from the woman, but the seat belt locked him in place. Another misting of blood spattered Tyler's face as Molly tore free from the young man's neck. Her mouth open wide and her eyes glowing a deep red. Tyler swore in the glint of the moonlight, he could see her canine teeth, elongated and dripping red like scalpels fresh from a surgery. The surreal moments of slow motion ended abruptly as they went over the embankment and into the darkness beyond.

They slammed into a dry creek bed. The car cascaded over the lip and headlong into a shelf of weather-beaten boulders and hard-packed dirt. Tyler and Tony both had their seatbelts on, and the airbags punched out at the moment of impact. Molly however, was still between the seats and untethered. She crashed through the windshield as the car met its sudden and violent end. Like a bag of meat and bones she crumpled into the rocks and split against the sand. Her body came to rest, twisted and broken in the smoking mass that was the front end of the car.

Tyler's head was spinning and the last thing he saw before he lost consciousness was her mangled corpse, and the form of his unconscious brother.

He woke in the hospital, his parents were there by his bed. He'd suffered two broken arms and a concussion but was otherwise intact. He asked about his brother as soon as he was able to speak. His parents shifted uncomfortably before answering, Tyler couldn't believe what they were saying.

Tony had had survived the crash, injured of course, but the truly bewildering part is that he had actually died as a result some sort of infection from the wound on his neck. It had spread through him rapidly and he was gone before anyone could help. Stranger still, apparently his body had gone missing shortly after being moved to the morgue. The coroner was found unconscious and Tony's body was gone.

The police and medical staff were eager to talk to Tyler about the accident. They kept looking confused when he brought up Molly though.

"Who's this girl you're talking about?" the detective asked.

"Molly, the dead one, she went through the windshield, her bag was in the back." He explained.

"Son, we didn't find any dead girl, or any bag. We did find a severed hand in the back of the car, though, that we are hoping you can explain."

Angel of Mercy

"You've come to kill me haven't you?" She asks without turning around, keeping her back to me. "It's okay. I'm ready."

Her thin arms pull a silk nightgown tight around her slender form as she stands silhouetted against the night sky. The bay windows before her are closed against the winter air, but the curtains are pulled back. Outside the window, a thin layer of snow covers tree tops as far as the eye can see. A full moon hangs swollen in the sky amid a bed of stars that shine like condensing diamonds against black velvet.

The sweat of my palm catches the cold air in the room and the knife I am holding grows cool in my hand. It had been a long hike out to the rural mansion. Despite the winter temperatures, the exertion had worked up a sweat under the layers of black winter-wear. After sneaking in and hunting my prey, I find her here in the library, looking out at the sprawling acres attached to the old Victorian manor.

My quarry is an old woman, whose name I have not committed to memory. I find it better not to learn my victims' names.

"I had hoped you'd come." She says.

Her voice is as frail as the rest of her, speaking up when I don't say anything. Still she doesn't turn from the window.

"There are jewels in the safe, if you've come to rob me. You can take anything you like. All I ask is you make sure I'm dead before you go. Please just don't let me linger… please don't let me survive."

This is not what I had expected. Every other victim I've claimed has cried, screamed, and fought for their life. People who are confronted with death behave erratically. They are rarely more alive than when confronted with the prospect of a violent end. Not her, however. She shivers against the cold, her breath fogging the glass in front of her like the growing shadow of a ghost on the clear barrier.

"I'm willing to help you make it look natural, though I admit I am not the expert here. I just… I've been ready to pass on for years now." She says, and finally turns to face me.

She doesn't look as old as I had expected. She's certainly well aged, maybe seventy or so, but a comfortable life has decreased the overall impact of the years on her. Her hair is pinned back, kept short, dyed, and shining in the moonlight. Her face is wrinkled, but mostly, it's just tired. She was a beautiful woman all her life, that much is clear, so much so that even now in the twilight of her years, she still has a certain ageless beauty.

I'm not sure how to respond. Usually when I'm this close to my victim, this feeling, something I call "The Surge", overtakes me. The hot rush of adrenaline and the thrill of the hunt turns my vision red. I get a fire inside that can only be quenched with pools of fresh blood. This time though, with her, that fire burns low. Something about this vulnerability and her expectant nature has disarmed me. It's uncomfortable and I start to sweat even more under the ski mask. She moves to the small cabinet over a mini bar at the side of the room. Even through all the layers, she sees my discomfort.

"Perhaps a drink? I can't imagine it was easy getting out here. I saw no car and none of the alarms were tripped. Though I've had a great many of them disabled. My home owners insurance won't allow me to turn them all off, you see. I do hope that wasn't too much trouble." She says with an ounce of regret.

She uses her delicate hand to wield a pair of gold tongs, dropping ice cubes into two crystal glasses, followed by two fingers of what appears to be brandy.

She brings one closer, not too close, but she sets it on the desk to my right and backs away. She sips her own and a slight wince crosses her features as she swallows.

"I'm nervous too." She offers, as though it would be some consolation. "But I'm ready. You see, my children were taken in a plane crash almost a decade ago. Both of them were on a flight here for Christmas with their families. A true tragedy in every sense of the word. My husband lost his fight with cancer just a few years ago. Besides this house and a bank account… I have nothing left. I have no surviving family to take my solace in, and I have no heirs or legacy to mourn me when I go. I'm tired and I don't want to be here anymore." She says, returning to the window.

I shift on my feet. If this is some sort of ploy to save herself, it's certainly buying time. I'm confused, and with the absence of The Surge I'm growing anxious. She watches me in the reflection of the window and smiles, sad but sweet.

"It's okay. We don't have to rush into anything and you are free to change your mind. I'd have done it myself but I have this fear of the afterlife…" Her hand comes to her chest, pulling a chaste silver cross from under her long nightgown. "I'm terrified of going to Hell. If you kill me now, I can go in peace. I can be done with it all. I can see my children, my grandchildren, and my husband. I've led a good life, and natural causes don't seem to be too eager to do the job."

I move to the table and pick up the drink, if for nothing else, to do something other than stand in the doorway, looming. There is no one else in the house, I made sure of that in casing the location. The serving staff comes out early and leaves late. The gate was open, and none of the exterior lights were on. Could it really be true? Was she really inviting this? Was she really inviting *me*?

This has to be some sort of game, yet, short of pulling a gun and shooting me, which it doesn't look like she has, there is nothing here that can save her. Unless she poisoned the brandy, in which case, she's drinking it too.

The mask covers my mouth and I lift it up, but that bunches it around my nose and eyes, making it awkward to drink. This causes her a small laugh.

"Oh please, you can dispense with that silly thing. In fact, if I see your face, you're required to do me in aren't you?" She asks and turns toward me with that same thin but genuine smile.

I can't argue her point and the mask is becoming stifling. The sweat and claustrophobic feeling just isn't the same without The Surge present. I am uncomfortable and unsure of myself for the first time since I can remember. I probably haven't been this nervous since my first kill. Even then, The Surge had propelled me. It had turned me into that animal that hides just below the surface. Now though… now it feels different. I peel the mask off.

"There we are. You know I hadn't expected that… I don't know what I had expected. You're a handsome young man." She says with a light laugh. She's shaking, but her amusement is genuine. "I can't imagine what has brought you to this but I'm glad it did, as horrible as that might make me to say it."

I can tell she is placating, or at least trying to. I've never been traditionally handsome. Wide set eyes, broad nose, cleft chin and a receding hair line. Perhaps in an old world sense of aesthetics, but not here in this day and age. Maybe her own years help influence it? Or maybe she is just disarming me? I sip the brandy, it's strong. It has a syrupy weight and a sugary taste on the front end of my tongue, but it is all burn and vapor on the way down. It warms my core, calms my jitters.

"I see you brought a knife." She says, her voice quivering. "Though I had hoped for something a little less.... Violent. I always imagined something that would seem like an accident. But I suppose one cannot be a beggar and a chooser. I do have something of a heart murmur, perhaps you could simply beat me about the chest a bit until it fails, and then toss me down the stairs? Maybe smothering with a pillow? Do you think that would work?"

I shake my head slowly, finally speaking. "That… only works if someone's breath is shallow enough…"

"I see." She sounds disappointed. "I had fond hopes of going in my own bed. Perhaps a poison? Though I don't imagine that is at all what you are hoping for either."

"I…" I falter when I start to speak, unable to really grasp how I am having this conversation with a victim. "I could bash your head in. Then down the stairs, like you said."

That causes her a shiver. "Yes well, I hear that can be quick, though the skull is stronger than most give it credit for. My husband took a nasty fall near the end. He caught his head on the kitchen sink. Split his forehead open, blood everywhere. I thought for certain there would be some brain damage but nothing of the sort. You must be thorough if that is how…"

She trails off, letting her voice fall into her glass.

"Strangling?" I ask, feeling absurd that we're now debating this. I've lost control in this scenario, and yet, I continue.

"I bruise easily… and I'd rather not make more trouble for you. I'm rich remember? There will be a lengthy investigation if foul play is involved. Without a husband or heirs, the lawyers will be fighting tooth and nail to get what I have and I'd rather not have my legacy be one of a murder victim. Which reminds me…"

She takes up a cocktail napkin and scribbles something onto it.

"This is the code to the safe under the bed, you'll find cash, and jewels so old they have no serial numbers. You should be compensated for your time and the risk."

What is happening right now? I flash back to my last victim, a single mother in a derelict apartment. Done up with a knife in her bedroom. I'd removed all the organs from her abdomen and heaped them onto the bed. The weight of them in my hands and the saturation of blood had soothed me. The man before her, a simple gunshot to the temple as he attempted to buy drugs from me in a parking lot downtown. That smell of gunpowder and the splatter of brains across his dashboard had been like birthday party confetti. Now this, whatever *this* was.

She sets the napkin down on the same table she had left my drink on.

"Well, I've no other ideas or preferences, I only ask that you not remove me from here… I can't bear the thought of just… vanishing or being a missing person. When the staff comes in the morning, they must find me dead, and in no way that will potentially implicate them." She says with a shrug. "Though I would prefer we get on with it before I come to my senses."

"I… have an idea." I say, finishing the drink and setting the glass down.

My thin leather gloves keep me from having to worry about finger prints. "You have a bathtub?"

"I do. A marvelous porcelain claw foot in the master bathroom." She says fondly, starting to see what I have in mind. "Should I go take a bath?"

"It's the best option I can think of. No one will question an old lady drowned in the bath, especially if she's had a few drinks." I say motioning the brandy.

"Now I know I'm in good hands." She says and finishes her drink, pours one more, and downs it in one quick swallow. She coughs, holding her chest a moment before she continues.

"It's just down the hall. When you hear the water stop, give me a few minutes and then we will detach."

I nod and step aside as she passes. She smiles to me, fondly this time. She lays a soft hand on my chest as she passes, mouthing a quiet “Thank you.”

I take my time in the library, lingering as I hear the water start, the sound echoing down the hall. It’s a strange feeling. I came in as an intruder and now I am not sure what I am. Some sort of hero? I try not to think on it too much as I fill the moments looking over old leather bound books with no titles on the spines. I find myself in front of the window, looking out at the acres sprawling before me. The tops of the trees reflect the moonlight up, like thousands of slender mountain peaks. It looks like some sort of Lovecraftian alien landscape. The glass is cold and I can feel it drawing the heat from my face. Thin tendrils of the chill cling to the sweat on my cheeks.

The sound of the rushing water stops and the hallway goes silent.

I pull my mask back on and take my time stalking down the hall. The old carpet is thick under my feet. The hallway lined with dimmed lights in ornate sconces. I make my way through the master bedroom, marveling at the antique four-post bed that serves as the centerpiece. Just beyond, the light of the bathroom spills out onto the floor. I creep closer, despite the lack of need for secrecy. I find it helps kindle The Surge as I start falling into the role. The talking is done, it’s time for the kill.

There she is, the back of her head to me, resting on the rolled edge of the huge tub. As promised it’s a perfect porcelain basin on bronze claw feet. The stone tiled floor shines brightly and on the marble counter top I see a half empty glass of brandy and an open bottle of sleeping pills. She has put more thought to this than I have.

I creep up behind her. The water is covered in a thick layer of heavy suds. It smells like lavender. My movement causes a slight refraction in the white tiles of the wall next to her and she shifts. Before she can look up, I grab her by the head and shoulders and force her under. A heavy wave of warm water rolls out and splashes across my boots, soaking my feet and pants. More follows as she starts to fight, with surprising strength. Perhaps she's reconsidered? Perhaps she's just filling the role? Either way, The Surge rolls strong within me and my grip tightens.

As she thrashes, the suds clear the surface of the water and I can see her naked old body underneath. She's kept herself well, though her skin is that classic "old person" skin, paper thin and showing thick blue veins throughout. She exhales one last yell from under the water and her body seizes and thrashes as she takes in a lung full of water. Her throat snaps closed as her body realizes that no air is coming in and her feeble hands on my wrist start to go slack. Even after she goes limp and her hands splash into the water, I hold her under.

When I finally step back, the soap bubbles start to settle once again, and obscure her form there below. I catch one last look at her face, her eyes half lidded, her mouth open wide, but there is a serenity to her there. She is at peace, and I feel like I've done something right, something heroic. I'm like an angel of mercy.

"Vacant Eyes" by Joel Greaves

Vacant Eyes

It was a dark and cold night in late December when little Holly Mae was tucked in to bed. She was almost ten, old enough not to need a bed time story anymore, but not so old as to turn down a goodnight kiss from both her mother and her father before the lights were turned out. She was loathe to admit however, she was not so old as to have done away with the familiar nightlight that was a fixture in the wall socket near her door.

Out on their farm house, they were no strangers to taking the full force of the elements and tonight was no exception. A smattering of rain pelted her window, and a steady wind shook the tree outside. The long shadowy fingers of the dancing branches cast themselves, outstretched and distorted, towards her bed. Though she had long come to recognize the shapes for what they were, she still had to roll away from the creeping tendrils of shadow. Instead, she preferred to face the wall next to her bed with her blanket tucked tightly to her chin.

Her mind wandered, as it often did in the haze before slumber, and as she started to drift off there came a sharp *CRACK!* against the window. Her eyes snapped open. She trembled, but odd sounds in the old house were not uncommon. It was nearly a century old. Plus, she was up on the third floor, about as safe as could be. It was probably just the trees hiting the window like they used to.

But…

Hadn't her father just pruned the tree this past summer? Maybe it was a bird that had flown into the window, lost in the storm, looking for shelter. Her heart broke a bit remembering when a bird had flown into the window of the den on the first floor. The poor thing had hit the glass so hard it broke its neck. She remembered vividly how it lay, twitching and flapping in the bushes. Her father had taken it to the barn and helped it find rest. They had a small funeral for it that evening in the garden.

CRACK!

Now she knew she had to get up and check. If it was a bird, she had to see. The sill outside her window was deep, it was possible it would have caught the bird if it had fallen. Cautiously, she crept out of bed to the window.

She peered out into the darkness, and saw nothing through the rain streaked glass. The gathering moisture formed long rows that looked like tears as they streaked towards the bottom. The tree branches were trimmed well away from her window, and whatever had made the noise would have fallen to the ground below. If it was a bird, there was nothing she could do for it now. She sat a moment, looking out at the barn and the dark expanse of fields beyond.

CRACK! Came the sound, right in front of her, loud and sharp and sudden. She almost fell back from the window. Her breath caught in her throat and she looked through the glass. This time when she peered out, she looked down, to see a blurred figure standing out in the grass apron that surrounded the house. The figure was still. So still she hadn't seen them at first. Despite the thin cloud layer, the moonlight was just bright enough to illuminate a simple white mask they wore. The eyes were pinched and beady, and the mouth was a long, amused smile.

Holly Mae screamed and ran to her bed. When her parents came in, she tried to tell them that she had seen a person in the yard. Someone in a mask. She was so scared, tears running from her eyes, that she couldn't properly articulate. Her father went to the window. Holly Mae watched him as he took a long moment looking out into the dark. He leaned forward and pressed a hand to the glass above his eyes to block the light of the room from obscuring his vision. Holly Mae held her breath, but nothing happened, and he straightened. Her mother stroked her hair and bid her to lay down. They assured her it was just a dream, they were miles and miles from anyone. They were safe. They were alone.

Holly Mae pulled her blanket up over her head once they left, trying to block out the rest of the world. She'd started to relax, started to contemplate sleeping once more, when it came again.

CRACK! The sound broke the peace of her room. She tightened her grip on the blankets and shrank further in her bed, trying to ignore it, to will that haunting image from her mind.

CRACK! It came again after a few moments then again, and again.

CRACK! CRACK!

Holly Mae called her parents again, too scared to move. Once more, they saw nothing. Her father assured her he would take a look downstairs and make sure everything was locked. She begged for him not to go. Her mother sat with her all the while, listening to her father thump around below. He was making a show of latching the deadbolt for the first time in years and doing the same as he locked the windows. His creaking foot steps up the two flights of stairs heralded his winded return. With another kiss, they were gone, assuring her the house was locked up, water tight.

With that, the light went out and all was quiet.

CRACK!

Holly Mae jolted hard in her bed, her muscles clenched.

CRACK!

The sound was not going to be denied. Holly Mae hid under her blanket but this time, they were not relenting.

CRACK!

CRACK!

CRACK!

Holly Mae jumped and shuddered each time… finally slipping out of bed and to the window, moving on her hands and knees. She hooked the tips of her fingers on the sill and ever so slowly raised her head up to peer out the window.

CRACK!

She flinched and ducked, waiting a few heavy breaths, her heart pounding and pumping like a piston in her chest.

She steeled herself and peered up over the ledge.

The masked figure was below, now close to the house. At the base of their porch, almost out of sight of the window, it stared up at her. The dark, empty eyes made the smile seem devious and startling to behold. With a flash of their hand, they threw another stone up at the window.

CRACK!

Holly Mae screamed and fell back from the window. She scrambled out of her room and down the hall to her parents' bedroom. Despite their protests, both her parents were convinced to go and look out her window, to see that horrible figure. She waited in their bed, shaking with anticipation. When her parents returned, seeing nothing alarming and certain she had a bad dream, she started to cry. They relented, allowing her to stay in their bed and she wriggled down in between them and lay tense and shivering until the sun came up.

When the rain stopped and the sun was finally up, she could hear their rooster crowing in the paddock and their cows calling for their morning grain. When the sun was fully over the horizon, Holly Mae braved slipping out of her parents' bed. Her mother and father began their waking process, their interrupted sleep making the morning heavy on their eyelids. She went first to her room. She held her breath as she neared the window. Nothing outside. Nothing in her room. It was quiet but the sunlight filtering in was warm and inviting, dispelling the fear and uncertainty.

She slipped down stairs, cautious, as she moved to the door that lead out to the porch. The sounds of waking life on the farm were comforting and she grew bolder with each slow step. She crept to each window and looked out the curtains, seeing nothing. She could see out across the pasture, no signs of danger. There were no signs of trespass or intrusion. Seeing that their house had been left at peace, she was finally feeling like things were back to normal.

That is, until she opened the door.

There on the doormat, staring up at her with vacant eyes, was that white, smiling mask.

Battle of the Band

“I’m telling you, cranking the engine didn’t work the last four hundred fucking thousand times, it’s not gonna work now!” Ricky yelled from the driver’s seat of the Ford Econoline van, currently half in the ditch of an unnamed desert road in the middle of exactly nowhere.

"Just fucking do it!" Jimmy barked from under the hood canopy, which was propped up as it had been for over an hour.

Ricky rolled his eyes, pushed his long black hair back, and sat forward. Turning the key caused the ridiculous amount of other keys on the bloated ring to jingle. As before, zero response. Not a click, thump, wheeze, chort, or grumble from the engine.

"Did you turn it?" Jimmy called.

"I'm fucking doing it!" He replied and as if in answer did it more violently and with exaggerated motion, as if to emphasize his action. He kept at it until the key ring came off in his hand, the key having snapped in the ignition.

"Oops." He said holding it up by the black nylon band. Embroidered in white letters were the words 'HAGRAVEN' and the logo of their band repeated down its length.

"Oops?" Jeremy sat up from the back, having been laying in the back, trying to tune them out, until that very moment. The heat of the day was causing beads of sweat to gather on his bald head. "What oops?"

"The key broke, man." Ricky said swinging it slowly like a hypnotist's pendulum. "In the ignition."

Jeremy looked confused, that is until blind anger over took his features. Ricky thought Jeremy was going to come over the seat at him and he flinched away. Instead, Jeremy went the other direction, out the back of the van. As he exploded out onto the sand, guitar cases, amps, speakers, drums, and other gear came rolling out with him. As so often happened, the chaos he was the cause of only made his temper worse. An amp smashed his foot, a snare drum banged against his knee, he almost tripped on a mic cable. Thus ensued a whirlwind of rage as Jeremy kicked and stomped and smashed in a frenzy of swearing and guttural yells.

Jimmy walked up to the driver's side window, looking to Ricky. He glanced towards the rear for a moment.

"Did you crank it?" He asked, ignoring the tantrum.

Ricky held up the key ring again.

Jimmy sighed. "Well that settles that. Good one."

"Hey, fuck off dude. It ain't my fault this key ring is packed full as fuck. I'm surprised Gene Autry didn't write a song about it."

Jimmy clearly missed the reference.

"You know," Ricky sang, poorly, he was the drummer after all. "*I got spurs that jingle jangle jingle.*"

Jimmy blinked slowly and walked towards the rear of the van, preferring Jeremy's cooling rage to whatever the fuck Ricky was on about.

Jeremy was fishing a cigarette from a smashed soft pack he kept in his breast pocket. He was getting low from the look of it, and that did not bode well for any of them. All tour there had been two things you didn't let run out: gas, and Jeremy's smokes. Now the van was broken down, and Jeremy was ripping through the last few he had. On top of that, the sun was going down.

"Well, looks like we're spending a night in the van." Jimmy said, surveying the damage done to his guitar case. "So I mean, this stuff needed to come out anyway."

Jeremy didn't say anything as he chewed on the back of his thumb, staring at a small dirt foothill adjacent to the road. Descending from the peak, they could see a black-clad figure picking their way down and towards them. That would be Laura, of course, having gone in search of a cell signal and to survey the land around them. Jeremy smoked his cigarette like he had a vendetta to settle with it, hoping beyond hope for some good news.

Behind them, Ricky hopped out from the van, slamming the door.

“Well now it’s officially fucked. I’m out of weed.” He announced, as though expecting an outcry of support.

Neither Jimmy nor Jeremy were listening.

“Did you hear me? There is no more ganja!” He announced again, coming around the back of the van.

“Oh hey it’s Laura.” He said sounding chipper and happy to see her, as if they hadn’t spent every day of the last two months in a van together.

Slowly but surely, Laura made her way back up to them, all three of them watching her. She was sweaty and red cheeked. Her red hair was damp and tangled, hanging in her face. She wasn’t the type of girl who saw the sun a whole lot in her normal life. She had certainly not planned on hiking in black jeans and combat boots.

"How'd it go?" Ricky asked, a sardonic up-tone in his voice.

Laura wiped her forehead, pushing her hair back, and moved to the back of the van. Thankfully they still had two gallons of water. She cracked one open and took a long chug, catching her breath.

"I think I got a call out to Richard, but reception was shitty and he is still at the booking office in LA. I tried to give him our last known location but then my phone died, because SOMEONE has been playing that fucking Tappy Tappers game." Laura said, glaring right at Jeremy.

"It's HAPPY Tappers and my clan is in the top ten for the whole world alright? I have to get my dailies in or we fall behind." He said, as though that obligation somehow made this whole scenario understandable.

"Anyone else's phone working?" Laura asked "I couldn't even see the highway from up there. There's nothing in any direction around here."

Jimmy shrugged. "It might be, but some fuck head in Louisville has it now and Verizon won't replace it until we get home."

Ricky also shrugged. "I've told you the fucking government is spying on us with those. I got rid of mine months ago."

Jeremy shook his head. "Mine's dead that's why I used yours for my game."

Laura sighed and took another drink. “And the van isn’t charging it…?”

Jimmy shook his head. “It has to be the battery or the alternator, or both. There is no juice at all in this rig. Nothing to the plugs, nothing to the engine. Just nothing.”

“Well fuck.” Laura said, sitting down.

“*And…*” Ricky said. “We’re out of weed.”

“FUUUUUCK!” Laura yelled, that little tidbit being the icing on the cake.

She flopped back into the empty space of the van floor behind her.

“Maybe someone will come down this road and help us.” Ricky said, stepping around the van to peer up and down the desert highway. It was like a long gray line extending to the horizon in either direction.

"No they aren't." Jeremy said, moving to sit on the bumper, glaring at Ricky. "This is all your fault."

"My fault? Please enlighten me how this is my fault." Ricky said, raising a brow.

"At the gas station, that old weirdo told us about this 'shortcut' didn't he? I told him to fuck off, but no. Just because he had a joint to smoke, Ricky thinks this guy is the best thing since Google-fucking-Maps. No one is coming down this road because anyone with any sense in their brain would avoid it."

Laura snorted, Ricky rolled his eyes.

"Bro, I checked the route, it's legit. I saved it on your phone, which you'd know if it wasn't as dead as

Euronymous after Varg put a knife in his face." Ricky replied.

"Well, whether it was here, or out on the highway the van was gonna break down." Laura said. "And bitching about it isn't going to help. We're fucked for now. We'll figure something out in the morning."

Jimmy nodded and started moving the rest of the gear out of the van. "Well we might as well get comfortable. I'm going to find something to start a fire, it's going to be cold tonight."

That night they started a small fire from sage brush, but that burned out fast, hot as it was. They tried some other bushes, but they didn't catch, and just smoldered. Finally, Jeremy hauled the spare tire out from the back, slashed it, and threw it on the cinders. No one thought it was a good idea, not even Jeremy, but once he committed to a bad idea, it was usually just best to let him get it out of his system.

"In the morning," Jimmy said as the tire started to burn, "We'll split up, two head back the way we came from, two head up the other way a few miles and see if there is anything we can find. Maybe on our own we can flag down a car. People probably are more likely to help one or two people than pull over for a gross van with four people on the side of the road."

The oily black smoke chased them all back from the fire. All except Jeremy, who had now fully committed to his new tire fire and was going to enjoy it. Plus he was out of cigarettes completely, and maybe hoping the rubber smoke would scratch that itch. It didn't, but he wasn't going to let anyone else know that.

"Well if we all go, what if someone shows up here?" Ricky asked.

"We'll leave them a note." Laura said, somewhat agitated.

Ricky continued, "Well I mean it will be hard for them to know when it got left, you know, someone... someone should stay back with the van, you know, all our stuff too, needs guarding."

"Look if your fat ass wants to stay here, that's fine. I'd rather walk by myself anyway." Laura shot back, stunning Ricky, his eyes going wide behind his glasses.

"Whoa... I'm just... thinking of our gear man. Remember that time in Atlanta?" He said, subdued.

Laura shook her head. “I’m sorry. I’m just getting really hungry. You know how I get when I’m hungry.”

Ricky waved it off. “I think we all do. I’m hungry too. We might have to like… draw straws and see who gets eaten, like Moby Dick and shit.”

“That movie was about a whale.” Jeremy said, coming up from near the fire, his face now streaked with black soot.

“It was actually a book.” Jimmy said, leaning on the van.

“And it actually was based off a real story and involved a bunch of sailors in a life raft, and they all draw straws to see who has to die, and who has to kill them. So these two best friends, like, one of them had to kill the other one so they could all eat him and survive. That's like us right now. Best friends, stranded with no hope of rescue who have to kill and eat each other to survive… heavy shit man." Ricky said, shaking his head.

Laura laughed. "Well, I mean you are the fattest one."

Ricky raised a brow. "Yeah but fat isn't good to eat. Contrary to popular belief. The fattest one isn't the best one to kill and eat."

Jeremy looked over to Jimmy. "Well, you're the oldest one so, you know, you've lived your life. Isn't that part of the rules? The old ones have to sacrifice themselves for the younger ones?"

Jimmy laughed. "Fuck no, I have wisdom and knowledge that can help get us out of this mess."

"Well don't wait for the big reveal on my account." Jeremy said with more than a little agitation. "That age and wisdom shit has done fuck all so far."

"Yeah, good call with the tire fire by the way." Jimmy shot back. "Solid plan. Nice and warm."

"It is!" Jeremy said defensively. "You'll be glad for it in about an hour."

"Yeah let me guess when we're cooking the unlucky son of a bitch we murder and chop up to eat."

"Well shit we CAN'T eat me." Ricky said. "I'm the drummer. Good luck finding a drummer while on tour, or anyone that can finish my tracks on the album."

They couldn't argue. Ricky had a point, for as much of a stoner and general smart-ass he was, he could perform blast beats and a solid double kick roll better than most drummers available.

"And I'm the fucking singer, this is MY fucking band." Jeremy said. "Pick someone else."

"Don't you dare say the fucking bass player. Don't you fucking dare." Laura said, and pushed to stand. "I work my ass off, plus I'm the only one that actually works the merch stuff *and* manages the website since you dumb fucks can't."

Another solid point, which left them all looking at Jimmy.

"Oh let me guess, everyone rally against the guitar player." Jimmy said with a laugh, though the laugh faded as the other three started to surround him. "Wait what the fuck are you guys doing?"

"We've replaced guitar players on the road before." Jeremy said, an ominous tone in his voice.

"And you have, like, the perfect mix of fat and muscle." Ricky said quietly.

"And you ARE the oldest one…" Laura said with a grin.

"Hey fuck you guys." Jimmy said, backing towards the van and grabbing his guitar case, pulling his Fender electric from it, and bringing it up like a proper axe.

"Look, I was just joking." Ricky said, his drum sticks coming out, twirling in his hands like a set of Japanese sai.

"I'm *not* joking. We gotta eat something." Jeremy said, picking one of his microphones up out of the dirt, twisting the cable around his fist like a garrote wire.

"Well fuck that I'm not gonna be the only one without a weapon!" Laura marched to the van and pulled out her bass guitar, though before she could get it fully free of the case, Jimmy rushed towards her, his guitar held high, and tried to bring it down across her back.

Laura was a strong girl though, and with the bass guitar half in its case, she spun and used her full weight to ram thc butt of the case into Jimmy's guts, causing him to double over and stagger back.

"Jimmy! What the Hell man!" Laura said, though he was unable to respond.

"Fuck you guys man!" He finally managed around gasping breaths.

Without warning, Jeremy rushed Ricky and caught him flat footed, swinging the microphone like a flail and crashing it against the drummer's cheek. Ricky staggered back, somehow staying on his feet. Jeremy came to follow up but misjudged the distance and threw a wild follow-up swing. Ricky tapped out a blast beat on Jeremy's face with the sticks and stunned him. Jimmy had another go at Laura, this time managing to swat her hard in the shoulder and neck with his guitar, making a comical *"Twang!"* sound.

"Owwwww…..! You asshole!" She snarled, turning as the pain washed over her.

"Oh fuck I'm sorry!" Jimmy said and let his guard down, only to have Laura stomp his foot with her combat boot, before she cranked her bass against his head. The loud *"Twong!"* of the strings vibrating could be heard over the fray.

Jeremy had managed to get the microphone cable around Ricky's neck, but one of the drum sticks had come up and was in the way, preventing him from truly strangling the big man and Ricky dropped straight back, kicking his legs out and smashing Jeremy between his bulk and the ground. The air went out of both of them and they rolled back into each other, grappling for supremacy. Jimmy rushed, pushing her back as he tried to tackle her. Blood was flowing from his nose and mouth as they went into the heap of bodies fighting there in the dirt.

It was impossible to sort the chaos there in the growing cloud of dust and pitch black smoke as it became a four way fight to the death. Laura scratched one of Ricky's eyeballs near clean from his skull. Jimmy bit most of Jeremy's ear off the side of his head. Ricky stabbed Jeremy in the thigh with a broken drum stick. Jeremy got the cord around Jimmy's neck and was pulling it tight before Ricky and Laura pulled themselves free, only to tackle into each other and tumble end over end towards the fire. Ricky was on top of Laura and about to stake her like she was a vampire, but Laura reached out and grabbed a handful of dirt from the fire pit, scalding the skin off her hand in the process. She threw the dirt into Ricky's face. He screamed as the super-heated sand blinded his one good eye and he fell back swatting at his face. Behind them, Jimmy managed to grab hold of the drum stick embedded in Jeremy's leg. He failed to dislodge it, and instead, started to twist it, causing Jeremy to yell out and slacken his grip for just a moment. Jimmy wiggled free and scrambled to his feet.

Jimmy was back up though he immediately started tripping on one of the mic cables. He twisted and spun, trying to keep his feet, but Jeremy was on him. He yanked the drumstick piece out of his leg and had raised it over his head. He stabbed it hard into Jimmy's neck, and then brought it out and stabbed it in again. Jimmy tried to fight Jeremy off, but it was no use. His screams grew wet. With a gurgling wail, he fell still. Jeremy stood there, bleeding from a handful of wounds, the one in his leg the most notable. His shoulders were heaving, and a tense quiet settled in to the desert air.

Ricky staggered over, somehow still able to see, if only barely. Laura was not long after, bloody and covered in dirt and soot from the fire.

"Jesus Christ, man…" Ricky said with a touch of irony.

An hour later, Laura, Ricky, and Jeremy were sitting around the fire. Jeremy was nibbling gristle off a femur bone while Laura was picking at an unidentified chunk of charred meat. The tire fire still stunk, but now it wasn't so bad. They had washed up as best as they could and used some of their merch to bind their wounds.

Ricky was full bellied and reclined back in the dirt, blood caked in his goatee and mustache. "You know, I was just kidding by the way. I really didn't think you were going to kill him, or anyone. I mean… bro… that was nuts."

Laura took a nibble then laid her meal back on the flat rock near the fire they were using like a caveman grill. "I mean yeah… I thought it was just a joke too... But you guys really went for it."

Jeremy stopped and looked to Laura. “What? I was starving. I saved *you* from starving.” He said hastily, pointing the femur at her, then going back to gnawing the bone.

“I mean we’ve only been out here what, like… six hours though. Were we really starving?” Ricky asked.

“Well now we’re definitely not. Who knows when help is going to come for us?”

It was then that the glow of head lights cast over them. A huge flat-bed a tow truck pulled up and stopped behind the van. The band shielded their eyes against the light as they looked on. Each of them was bloody, filthy and streaked with black soot from the fire.

From the passenger seat of the tow truck, their manager, Richard, climbed out and fanned the plumes of tire smoke out of his face.

“Hey team! I got Laura’s message. I’m sorry I… God dammit you guys! Not again...”

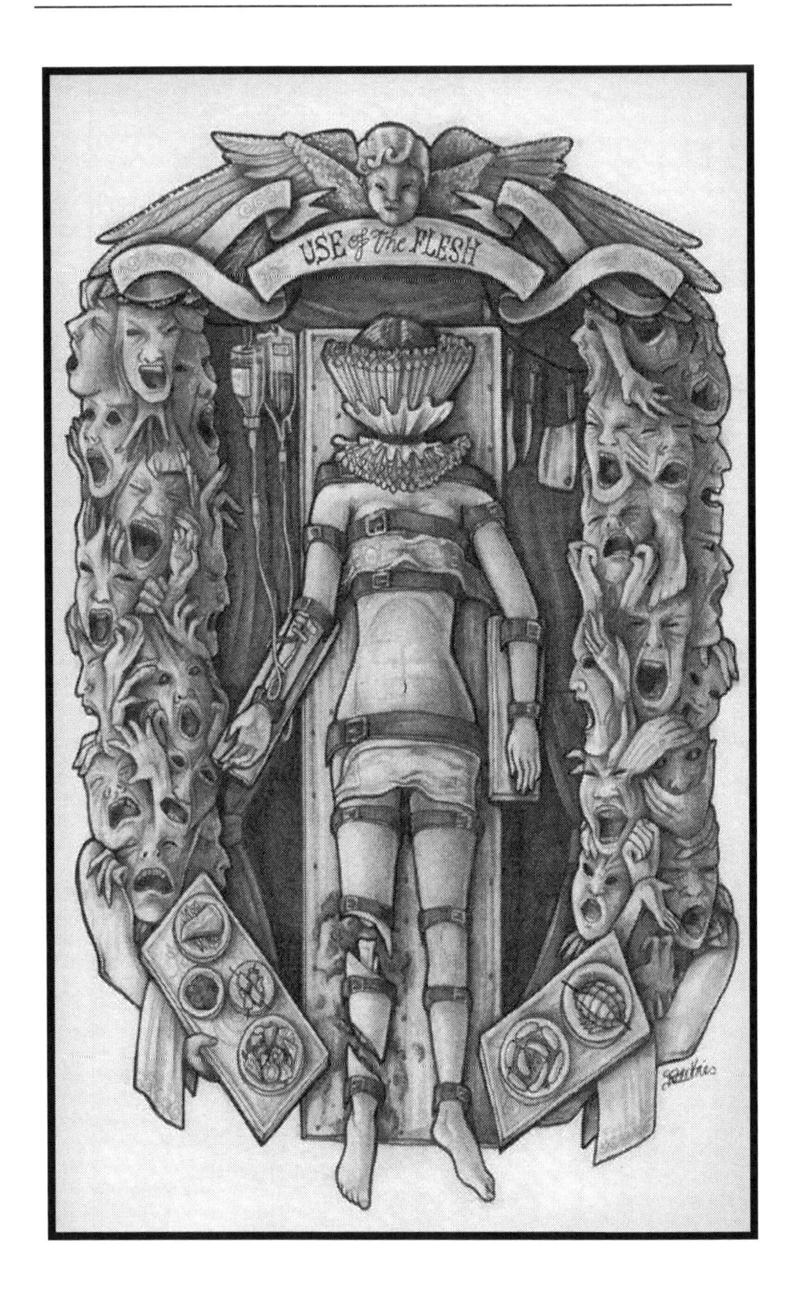

"Kammy Luv" by Sylvia de Vries - Ribbers

Cannibalia – A Novella

"If this place is so swanky, how come it's all the way out here? Everything for the last two miles looks like crack houses and serial killer shacks…" Chloe asked from the passenger seat of Owen's red Maserati.

It was brand new, and 2050 had been a great year for the sports car. It was sleek and efficient, with touch pad interfaces more akin to a spaceship than a passenger vehicle. The turbo charger on the engine sang then sighed with each buttery smooth shift of the car's auto pilot.

Chloe checked her makeup in the mirror for the hundredth time. She spent a few moments teasing her auburn hair back from her face and making sure her full lips were detailed and looking extra pouty. She adjusted her V-neck top in the mirror, making certain her ample cleavage was symmetrical and well displayed.

The slim LED lights in the panels provided just enough of a glow for Owen to navigate his breast pocket and withdraw a slim black case. From within he drew a long red cigarette and touched it to the filament on the corner of the container, causing the end to spark to life. He huffed the smoke to life, oily rolls of white smoke pluming down his front. He slid his finger over the car's touch console, and turned the volume of the music down.

"Because, like I told you, this place is hardcore underground. Elite. Crème de la crème. Special invitation only. I had to pull a lot of strings to even get you in the door, but I think you're going to dig it. Being seen here? Could really help your career. You know Dutch Coronado?"

"Umm who doesn't?" Chloe asked sardonically. "Are you saying he'll be there?"

"He'll be there. His boss will be there, his boss' boss will be there. You want to make it in this town? You're about to rub elbows with fucking royalty 'Lo." Owen punctuated each syllable with the red cigarette as he spoke, the silvery smoke almost spelling out the words for him.

"Ugh, I told you not to call me that. I'm trying to build a brand, I'm not fifteen and we're not in Kentucky anymore."

"Okay fine, *Chloe.* You know your mom is going to be crushed that you're not using your real name. Loretta." He said with a sly grin as the car merged around debris in the dilapidated freeway without breaking stride.

"*You* will be crushed if you call me that again." She warned and snatched the cigarette from his hand.

She took a long drag, which caused her to cough dryly.

"Hey watch the interior!" Owen said with a laugh, taking the it back before she could drop it and burn his upholstery. “I bet that hurt. When was the last time you smoked?”

“Like three months now.” She said, her voice hoarse. She thumbed open the tab on her water bottle, the micro filter in the mouth piece whirring to life as she drank. “It doesn’t help that you got sold some garbage Shift.”

“Hey this Shift is top notch. I got it from Rico’s guy. It’s fucking ninety eight percent pure.” He said with a puff. “You’re gonna be fucking *shif-ted.*”

He emphasized the syllables, each time punctuating with the end of the Shift cigarette.

Chloe cleared her throat and sat back in the seat, feeling the warmth behind her eyes start to spread. Shift was usually a slow burn high, but this one felt more like a bonfire in her brain. Her low tolerance and the apparent strength of the drug meant this might have been a mistake. She tapped into old party instincts and breathed in deep, and slowly out.

"You gonna be okay?" Owen asked with a laugh.

"Fuck off. Just gimme a minute. Turn up the music. I fucking love this song." She said, closing her eyes a moment. She laid her head back against the firm headrest. She pulled a little slack from the seatbelt, causing the sensor in the car to chirp a scolding tone at her from the readout.

Owen laughed and slid a finger over the readout, causing the music to pump through the twelve point surround sound system with operatic crystal clarity. The musical act *'Kammy Luv and the Teenage*

Heartache' was singing out their angst-ridden lyrics over a dance club beat. Kammy had been all the rage when Chloe was in high school, having been at the top of the charts for weeks at a time. Her music video for the song, *'My Heart is the Moon'* was the first video to reach one trillion views on the streaming neural net site ViewTube.

Nowadays though, Kammy was starting to show her age and was losing her grip as the Queen of Pop. She still got plenty of air time, and Chloe still loved her older tunes. She'd even won a talent contest for singing Kammy's version of *'Somewhere Over the Rainbow'* from the classic movie *'The Wizard of Oz'*.

Chloe let her mind drift out the window over the cityscape. The Shift flared her pupils and allowed the lights of the city to sparkle in. The derelict warehouses and shipping yards around them were wreathed in refracted rainbows. The heaps of rubble and detritus of civilization along the ghostly freeway no longer seemed so sad. The vibrations of the road caused the cells of her body to slither and dance against one another, resulting in a warm tension, a sort of pleasant anxiety, that washed over her. She was eager for something to happen, and yet sedate at the same time. The feeling of being an observer in her own mind was accurate as the Shift kept her displaced in time.

Owen flicked the butt of his cigarette out the window and laid his hands on the wheel. Disengaging the auto pilot, helaid on the gas. The warning chime of the car came again, advising against such high speeds with potential impact danger ahead, but Owen dismissed the warning as they sped out away from the clustered lights of the city.

As the Shift started to settle out and that displaced feeling of being outside her own mind faded, Chloe realized they were well outside the designated safe zone of the city. They were out in the chaotic wastes of the no man's land between metropolitan security check points. The landscape was dark in all directions, save for directly in front of them where the LED lights of the car spread a cone of visibility out on the landfill.

"Where the fuck…" She asked, though her throat was dry.

She plucked her water bottle from the cup holder and cracked the seal.

"I told you it was a ways out. Don't worry, we're almost there." Owen smiled, weaving through derelict abandoned cars.

"Almost where…?"

"The middle of nowhere."

Sure enough, Owen downshifted the car and veered off an old exit ramp. The signs had long rusted off their poles, giving her no indication just how far they had traveled.

He dimmed the lights of the car as they navigated through the wasteland. Chloe swore she could see eyes in the darkness looking out at them, but that might have been the lingering paranoia of the Shift. Owen seemed perfectly at ease as he quieted the music. They came around a bend, and Chloe could see a long row of nice, new cars all parked neatly in a row, bumper to bumper.

Amid the cars were several armed men in black suits, flanked by hefty SUV's with flood lights that lit them up as they pulled in. Chloe could feel the butterflies in her stomach turning into eels and then knotting themselves around one another.

"Owen you need to tell me what's going on..." Chloe whined from the passenger seat.

"Don't worry. We're cool. Hand me the black envelope from the glove box."

She blinked and leaned forward, popping open the compartment and producing the small, greeting card sized envelope. Before she could examine it, he snatched it from her hands and rolled down the window.

“Private party tonight. You have an invitation?” A guard asked as he came up alongside the car.

His face was obscured by the shine of his flashlight.

“Yessir.” Owen said, sliding a thin, silver-laden card from the envelope.

The invitation disappeared into the flare of light. There was a long quiet moment before the light motioned and the invitation came back into view. Owen took it and slid it into the breast pocket of his jacket.

“Park down at the end, the ferry leaves in five minutes. Next one is in thirty, so if you don’t want to wait, you better get moving.” The guard said as he directed them with his flashlight before he moved on towards another pair of headlights that appeared behind them.

Owen rolled his window up and drove down the row of cars, parking the small sports car with ease and killing the engine.

“Bring your jacket. The ride out is chilly.” Owen said as he pulled another Shift cigarette from its pack.

“Ride out where?” Chloe asked, frustration lacing her voice. “You haven’t told me shit, Owen, and this is getting fucking weird.”

“We’re going on a… cruise. Think of it like that. Don’t worry, we’ll be back before dawn.” Owen said, cracking his door and climbing out.

The dome light washed the night vision from her eyes, almost painfully. Chloe reached behind her seat, and pulled out her wool coat as she climbed out of the car.

The smell of a wharf at low tide hit her like a baseball bat. The stench of rot was oily in the air. Not of any one thing, but of many combined organic things all lumping together and decaying into one feculent organic paste. She was glad when the Shift smoke from Owen's freshly kindled cigarette hit her nose, almost burning it away. Almost. She was sure these clothes, and especially her open toed shoes, were a poor choice.

She didn't dare a look down as she stepped in something soft when she came around the car to join Owen. She could hear the slow and steady roar of waves nearby, indicating that they were along the shoreline. The sea air grew colder as they moved around the dunes that were comprised of pure garbage and were exposed to the direct wind coming off the water. The fresh air was a relief, though the acidic smell of alkaline and rust from the water was more noticeable out here than in the city.

She could see a string of party lights ahead of them and a small but new-looking pier jutting from the beach out into the surf. At the end of it waited a small boat, which was just starting its engine. It had a humble roof on it but it was largely open air. On board were several other couples, all dressed in their finest, and with heavy coats pulled around their shoulders. They were talking quietly and shared a laugh as Chloe and Owen approached. The pilot of the boat acknowledged them and bid them to board and sit.

Owen helped Chloe on and led her to the bench seat, sliding in next to an older couple that Chloe recognized, though she wasn't sure from where. The man had graying hair and the hints of wrinkles at the edges of his eyes and chin. His eyes were a striking gray and his smile and nod were practiced and polite. The woman next to him had recently dyed her hair, an artificial looking auburn that seemed out of place on her slightly withered features. She hardly gave Chloe a second glance as she looked out to the darkened horizon as the boat pulled away from the pier.

"First time out?" The older gentleman asked, and as soon as she heard his voice, Chloe placed him.

She recognized him from his campaign commercials that had played during the election season. She was sitting next to United States Senator, Harrison Aines. She felt her mouth go a little slack as she realized. She looked around the boat, and though she didn't recognize anyone else, she realized the caliber of company they were in. Her mind raced through the possibilities as they sped out across the open water.

"Second for me, first time for my friend here." Owen said, touching his chest with a hand before offering it to the other man. "Owen. This is Chloe."

The senator shook it politely, then Chloe's in turn when she offered her hand.

"Well I hear they have something quite special planned for tonight." Aines said, remaining cordial.

"I hear they always do." Owen laughed, which tugged a smile to the corners of Senator Aines' mouth.

"Very true." He said, reclining back, his wife shouldering in next to him against the cold sea wind.

Chloe pulled her own coat in tighter. The bounce of the boat, combined with the euphoria of the Shift was starting to turn her stomach. Luckily, Owen had told her not to eat before they came out, she was glad for that now.

It was the better part of an hour before they saw the lights of the luxury ship on the horizon. They all turned excitedly to face it. Everyone's cheeks and noses were red from the barrage of cold, hard air, and Chloe could feel her lips starting to chap, despite the fresh application of lipstick. Her toes were numb and her legs were stiff and sore from the cold.

The small talk around the boat had stopped long before, and now with relief in sight, everyone started to warm up once again. The boat pulled into a small bay at the back of the ship, and tethered there. A gangplank was lowered by members of the ship's crew. One of the crewmen made the momentarily precarious trip down to the raft to secure the plank. Once it was locked in place, he started helping people, one by one, up onto the ship.

Owen prompted Chloe to lead and followed her up the plank. She was cold through, her legs and butt were sore enough that she had to stop and lean on the rail once they made it to the deck. She made a show of acting like she was looking at the miles of black roiling water around them, while the feeling and strength returned.

"Come on 'Lo, I'm freezing out here. I hear music and I smell champagne. Let's go."

"Don't fucking call me that." She said, trying to sound mad, but she was wide eyed and scared.

She clung to Owen's arm as he followed the signals of the ship's crew that directed them up a flight of stairs. They were battered by a sudden sting of icy rain that felt like they were being pelted with thumb tacks. They were exposed only for a second as they finally found respite behind a set of double doors. Chloe breathed a sigh of relief as they got in out of the wind.

As her eyes adjusted to the change in the lighting, she was pleasantly surprised to find that the interior of the upper deck was a stark contrast to the rusted hull of the exterior. Wood paneling adorned the walls with deep red velvet curtains framing coat racks and shelves for people to check their bags. The soles of her shoes sank into a lush carpet that matched the red velvet trim of the room.

Everyone was lining up at a small counter, exchanging their coats and bags for small white tickets. The transaction was handled by a short stocky man in a suit. He seemed pleasant enough but he kept the knot of his tie jerked down sloppily and the top button on his collar was vented open. As they made their way closer, Owen leaned over to her, speaking quietly.

"Leave your phone and wallet in your purse, check everything. Every. Thing. We'll be fine but security is no joke, don't even try to test it okay?"

"Jesus Christ, Owen… what the fuck is this…?" She asked.

She was getting frustrated, but not eager to be out in the cold night air again. She buttoned up her purse, slid out of her coat, and handed both to the attendant. He nodded and dumped her items into a cubby that had a corresponding number to the ticket he provided her.

"Just like I promised, dinner and a show. You wanted to rub elbows with the upper crust? Well get ready." Owen said as he accepted his own ticket from the attendant.

He took her arm in his and led her to the line that was filtering through an ornate set of double doors. Once there, Owen handed over the silver invitation. This time, it did not come back to him. The man at the door examined it thoroughly and slid it into a heavy looking iron box on the wall. He waved them through and looked on to the next people in line.

Chloe started to see more details filtering into her vision as the chill cleared, and the haze from the boat ride finally shook free. The shelves around the entry way were carved with cherubic angels all seeming to hold the wood aloft in a tangle of fat bodies and tiny wings. Each of their faces was a mask of sadness, and instead of eyes, whoever had carved them had only left two smooth divots, no eyes or sockets to be seen. Around the frame of the door, what appeared to be wood grain at first, showed itself to be equally ornate carvings of countless faces and hands all appearing to be frozen in masks of pain and anguish sunken into the lacquered wood. Like some torturous abyss, each one having been trapped while trying to claw their way free of their two dimensional prison. Above the door the words '*Use of the Flesh*' were carved in calligraphy lettering.

Chloe shivered as they neared, and clung to Owen. Everyone in the line, the Senator from the boat included, were all pleasant and cordial but it was clear everyone was eager to get through. The general buzz of social greetings and congenial small talk was like static around her, all of it audible but none of it decipherable. Owen kept her arm in his, his free hand in his pocket. His posture was straight and his eyes scanned the crowd as they passed through the ornate wooden door.

Coming out the far side, they found themselves in a long banquet hall. That same dark grained wood and deep red from the lobby spilled through the door behind them and extended out in all directions. Deep red carpet, matching table cloths, and thick curtains that extended from floor to ceiling. Every surface was real wood, old and polished to a shine. The rods and alcoves that framed the curtains on the walls were adorned with more of those smooth-faced, eyeless cherubs. Chloe wasn't sure what it was about them that set her so ill at ease. They should have been cute, but they were like deformed children with wings. Not exactly wholesome décor. At least it was warm, and they finally had some elbow room as they came free of the tangle of people and filtered to the outskirts of the room.

Owen continued to scan the crowd, though before she could ask what he was looking for, Owen was signaled by a dashingly handsome man with silver hair, blue eyes and cheekbones that could cut glass. Owen smiled and led her over.

"Declan!" Owen called as they neared, and the two men embraced in a brief, comradely hug.

"Owen, my man. I was worried you wouldn't show." Declan said, as they parted the hug, though Declan kept a firm, friendly hand on the man's shoulder.

"Wouldn't miss this for the world, not after last year. I'm hooked." Owen said, his smile broad and easy, the kind of smile he only ever got when he was genuinely excited.

"And who's your date?" Declan said, turning his full attention to Chloe.

Chloe felt her heart flutter when her eyes met Declan's. He was wearing a perfectly fitted silk suit and a pink under shirt that was unbuttoned at the collar. On anyone else it would have made him look like a porno director, but somehow that trace amount of sleaze was just as tasteful as the expensive cologne that was permeating the area around him.

"This is my best friend in the whole world, Chloe Merwyn. Singer, actress, author. This one does it all Declan, total package." Owen said, nudging Chloe forward, encouraging her to take Declan's out stretched hand.

Chloe had to fight to summon up the practiced grace and demeanor she had been cultivating so diligently. After a long heartbeat, she flourished the smile she had been told broke more hearts than Country music. She laid her fingers gently into his hand and Declan, didn't miss a beat in placing his lips to the back of her knuckles.

"Declan Romero. Owner of Palladia Records." He said, in such a way that told her that single phrase had gotten this man more ass than a toilet seat.

What should have been a red flag to her, instead blossomed as a tingle in her stomach and thighs.

"Charmed." She offered, with a single flick of an eyebrow before she removed her hand. "And this is?"

Chloe deflected with a nod to the eye candy on Declan's flank, a tall woman in a velvet dress who appeared bored at the introductions. She was wearing a long black velvet dress and her short black hair framed her face in perfect symmetry.

"Oh shit. Forgive me, this is Amada Kamarov." He said stepping aside as the woman came forward as her lips parted into a strained, but lovely smile.

"The pleasure is mine." Amada said with a strong, slow voice that was wrapped heavily in an intoxicating foreign accent, though she offered no hand or gesture of greeting.

Chloe could see a flash of disdain in her eyes behind the practiced façade. Chloe wondered if she was some sort of client or call girl. It didn't matter, and

Chloe didn't have time to contemplate it as Declan lead them to a table near the side of the room.

As they moved, Chloe could see all of the seats in the room were facing the same way, leaving long sides of the tables empty. At the far edge of the room was a raised dais, like a circular stage surrounded by more of those cascading red velvet curtains. They spilled down from the ceiling above, pooling around the floor of the stage.

Owen pulled her chair for her, and she slid into it, thanking him with a curt nod. Owen hardly noticed as she sat, both he and Declan were wasting no time launching into animated conversation. That was to say, Declan started into animated conversation, mainly about money, cocaine, pussy, exotic locations, fast cars… The man was an orated copy of Hustler and Owen was gobbling it up, hook, line and sinker.

Owen's body language told Chloe she was a ghost to him, his full attention on his silver haired man-crush. That was fine, it gave her a shield from the room as she leaned in against him and looked out at everyone taking their seats.

To say the people in attendance were 'A-List' was an understatement. She recognized a dozen faces from TV, movies, magazines and beyond. She was two tables over from Jeremy Grummond, the teen star turned indie film director. Across the aisle was Catherine Majors, the Oscar winning actress from the classic film *'Never Was She Ever'*. Sitting next to her was freshly paroled actor turned eco-terrorist, Blaine Pierce. She was sure she even saw the guy who voiced the talking frog in the animated kids movies that made over a billion dollars every year. Whatever his name was. The combined net worth of just the people she could identify was enough to buy the entire continent of

South America, it seemed. In addition to the faces she could see there, there were people around the room wearing elegant, white half-masks. They obscured the upper portions of their faces while leaving their mouths uncovered. They were all similar to what she could recall from *'The Phantom of the Opera'*.

She couldn't imagine the turmoil if something were to happen to this ship. The aftershock ripple of Shift gave her a slight giggle, and soon gave way to a chill, though she couldn't quite nail down where it came from. She tried not to get caught staring and thought it the perfect time to practice her disaffected and bored demeanor. She called it her 'heiress affectation'. She could see it on many faces in the room, including Amada, who hadn't said a word since they sat down.

She could see puffs of cigarette smoke popping up like mushroom clouds among the crowd, and the smell started to permeate the air. As oppressive as it was, it was a human smell, and helped bring her back to reality. Above them, the house lights dimmed and there was an excited buzz that sent a vibrating hush over the room. Finally Owen pulled out of orbit around Planet Declan and squeezed her leg under the table.

She grabbed his hand tightly and refused to let it go. She smiled over to him and caught Declan leering down the front of her dress. She was grossed out but given who she was and where she was trying to go, she decided to let him get his fill and maybe he'd like what he saw.

Soon however, even Declan's eyes were pulled to the front of the room as the house lights dimmed further, and the lights on stage came up fully. From behind the curtain came a slender old man in a crisp tuxedo, complete with sharp bow tie and a jacket with coat tails that hung down near to the backs of his knees. His gray hair was slicked back with pomade and perfect to behold. The crowd fell quiet as he waited, wearing a beaming and patient smile on his face.

"Good evening." He said in a clear voice that was mic'd up through the house speakers.

"Welcome, one and all, to the Feast of the Golden Calf. We celebrate our one hundred and fourteenth year on the good ship '*Atreus*'. I see many familiar faces. But to those who are new," He let the words linger in the air, his eyes seeming to lock onto Chloe's there in the dark for just a moment before he continued.

“To those who are new; you are in for such a delight. A world class, one of a kind meal. The likes of which you have never seen and may not be prepared for. I implore you, keep an open mind. I am certain, like everyone else in this room, you will see the beauty of tonight’s festivities. And if not, well, we are on international waters and good luck prosecuting anyone in this room!”

He punctuated his last statement with a sharp, derisive laugh, one that echoed out across the room.

“Snitches get stitches!” Declan called and slapped the table, almost knocking over a flute of champagne that had been placed before him.

Chloe was startled to see she, too, had a flute of the golden sparkling libation before her. She had not seen it delivered, or if she had, it was lost in the stream of questions all clogging up her thoughts.

"Now, without further ado. The toast." The Host said, raising his own glass elegantly in a delicate, gloved hand.

When he lifted his glass, everyone rose their own, Chloe following suit.

"Gather us round, our plates of opulence. With gilded forks and sharpened knives we feast on the flesh of divinity, and know with certainty, that we taste the wealth of God." He said in a somber recitation.

He tipped his glass to the room and brought the flute to his lips, taking a sip. The room followed suit. Both Declan and Owen drained theirs in one swift swallow. Chloe and Amada were both more reserved in their delicate sips. It was delicious but something in the man's opening ceremony had her stomach twisted into a knot as tight as an iron padlock.

The Host drained his flute much slower, but he exhaled a sigh of satisfaction, smacking his lips and pondering the glass a moment before he looked to the room with a smile.

"Bon appetit." He said with a smile and moved off into the shadow that flanked the rounded stage.

Chloe saw the curtain start to pull to the side and she quested for Owen's hand under the table, clutching it tightly again once she found it. The curtain slowly crept aside, gathering in around itself and tucking away into the darkness. The lights focused in on a young woman, sleeping in a hospital bed. A tree of

IV tubes was branched into her arm, full bags hanging swollen with various fluids.

Once the curtain was out of the way a team of two nurses and a doctor, complete in scrubs, hair nets and face masks, came out onto the stage and started checking the woman. Heart monitors started to beep and the gentle suck and woosh of a respirator could be heard. General conversation started to grow with a tone of excitement. A blood pressure cuff buzzed and then vented as the monitors alongside the bed started to light up with information.

A sudden slap on the table startled Chloe back into her chair as Declan laughed and called out.

"Kammy Luv!? You're kidding me. That's Kammy Luv!" He laughed looking between her, Owen, and Amada.

"Seren-fucking-dipity," Owen laughed. "We were just listening to her on the way out here."

"What are they doing?" Chloe asked, staring at one of the most influential pop starlets on the planet, being triaged and treated like she was in an operating room.

"You didn't tell her?" Declan asked, half laughing, sounding genuinely amazed.

"Tell me what?" Chloe asked, her eyes narrowing.

"Well no, I mean you know the rules." Owen said, defensive but still grinning.

That actually caused Amada to give him a scathing look and she said something under her breath in a language that sounded like Russian or Romanian.

"Tell me *what*?!" Chloe insisted, raising her voice, drawing a few looks from the people at the adjacent table.

"Just watch." Owen said, holding a finger to his lips to hush her.

Chloe fumed, her cheeks growing red, but the eyes of people on her cowed her back into her seat once more. Tobin Frank, one of the biggest directors in Hollywood, and his wife, were watching her quietly. Chloe forcibly regained a measure of her composure, and fell quiet.

Once the monitors and IVs were all running, Kammy was carefully restrained down to the bed with thick Velcro straps across her chest, arms, and one holding her head in place. The foot of the bed was lowered, and the head of it brought upright, until

Kammy was all but standing. Still restrained and looking like a sleeping angel there, with her shimmering dark hair draped over her shoulder, and wings of monitor cables and IV tubes backlit by the ambient stage lights.

The nurses knelt down and rolled the bed sheet up, exposing the entirety of Kammy's leg, from her dainty toes, all the way up to the shapely curve of her rump. Her stomach and groin were carefully and deliberately obscured by a sheet, which was then pinned in place, preserving some sterility and modesty in the exposure. Her caramel colored skin was illuminated as a sharper white light beamed down from above. A tray of surgical implements was rolled over. Though Chloe couldn't see what was on the tray, the doctor made a show of picking up each implement and inspecting it in such a fashion that the crowd could get a look. Scalpel, forceps, bone saw; all cold stainless steel and shimmering in the light.

As the doctor looked over the tools of his trade, another set of long tables was rolled out by the wait staff into the open area before the stage. Two of the long tables were laden with cutting boards, plates, knives, and dishes of all shapes and sizes. The center table appeared to have a grill of some type, which was confirmed by the propane tank hooked up underneath.

More champagne was poured and a general chatter of excitement circulated through the room. Chloe has a sick feeling bubbling in her stomach as the wait staff was replaced by kitchen staff, signified by checkered pants and long white canvas coats buttoned at the shoulder. They even had the tall cloth hats on their heads. The cooks all went about cleaning and preparing their tables and stations, chopping vegetables, firing up the burner and organizing the new 'second stage'.

The concert of nurses prepping a patient, and the chefs prepping a kitchen was painting a clear picture to Chloe, though she stubbornly refused to put the equation together, despite the clear symbiosis on the upper and lower productions. It was a paradoxical comparison, but the similarities were clear, each group cleaning, sterilizing, and sharpening. Though one apparently for surgery, the other for a banquet. Chloe felt like she was going to throw up.

The Host stepped out from the curtain once more, carefully moving around the nurses as he spoke up.

"Well I don't think our guest of honor needs any introduction. She started as an adorable starlet on *'The*

Bruno Bird Show' when she was just six years old. She's the youngest Oscar nomination for Best Supporting Actress in history. Her albums have topped both billboard charts and international sales records. With a combined net worth of over eight hundred million dollars… The one and only, Kammy Luv."

He spoke as one of the nurses pushed a syringe of something into the IV bag. Kammy stirred gently and half woke, moaning. Apparently she was mic'd up, too, as the soft, almost bird-like noises came over the speakers.

"'*Good morning Starshine'*…" The Host said in an extremely dated pop song reference. "'*The Earth says hello'*."

Despite the ancient joke, a small titter went out through the room. Kammy roused a bit further as another nurse moved close and affixed a wide Elizabethan collar around her neck. It was small, but looked like something a veterinarian would put on a dog to keep them from chewing on a wound. Her face was still visible, but it was clear that Kammy couldn't tilt her head down nor see anything below her delicate chin. Chloe didn't like that implication any more than she liked the idea of a buffet being prepared at the singer's feet.

"Hi… I'm really thirsty…" She said in a high, thin voice.

She sounded like a child with the flu being cared for by a doting parent.

"Of course." The host said motioning for a steel cup with a thin straw protruding from the top. "But just a sip. Doctor's orders."

That got another light chuckle from the crowd. He held the straw up to her to have a brief drink before he set the cup aside. Kammy laid back with a contented sigh, moaning gently as a wave of drug-induced euphoria washed over her.

"Fuck, I swear I could jerk off to that sound." Declan said to Owen, despite not taking his eyes off the stage.

"Tell me about it…" Owen said, a dreamy quality to his voice.

Chloe could feel her fondness for Declan's sleazy charm starting to give way to revulsion. Her shock at Owen's similar behavior was also palpable, but was taking a back seat to the horror of the scene unfolding before her.

"Owen, please tell me they aren't going to…" She started, but Owen brought a finger to his lips once more as the Host motioned to a side door along the stage.

"And introducing Kammy's date for the night, a graduate of the American Culinary Institute of New York and a fixture on the cooking competition reality show, *'Master Chef'*; Hernando 'Nando' Castillo."

A young man, similarly dressed to the other staff, stepped out from the door to a round of applause. His chef's hat was draped back over his neck and his sleeves were rolled up, showing a sleeve of tattoos on either arm. His thin mustache was twisted up at the ends in a way that focused the features on his round face. He wasn't fat, but was certainly soft around the edges.

Nando was met with polite, but genuinely exuberant applause. He raised his arms to the crowd, waving and smiling ear to ear as he moved to the wash station that had been set up, and made a show of scrubbing his hands. As he dried his hands he looked over the various preparations being done. He walked the row of tables, watching the other cooks begin their prep work. The surgeon on stage began to do the same; once more, their work seemingly concerted and eerily similar in their finer points.

Just behind the raised dais, Chloe could see more ambient stage lighting come to life, softly illuminating a small twelve piece orchestral band. There was a soft moment of tuning, turning the scene before them into an intimate preparation. Like a "behind the scenes" glimpse they were all privy to.

Nando took up his own kitchen knife and ran it over a whetstone. The surgeon on stage washed up as well, and his nurses moved over to place his gloves and apron on. He then took up his scalpel and moved alongside Kammy.

"No, no. Fuck no. Owen…" She whined quietly.

Owen squeezed her leg. Hard. The look on his face was one of both anger and fear.

"Relax 'Lo." He said, hissing through clenched teeth. "Fucking. *Relax*."

He reached into his coat pocket and pulled out one of his red Shift cigarettes. He was casual and smiling but kept that tight grip on her leg. Declan and Amada were watching the activity on the stage, though

Amada graced her with another of those icy side-long glances.

Owen lit the cigarette and took a deep drag and offered it to Chloe.

"Owen no, I…" She started but he pinched her leg and thrust it at her once more.

"Smoke it. You need to chill out." He said, exhaling the oily smoke. "You need to chill out, like *now*."

Declan raised a brow. "Oh shit, I haven't been shifted in a month. Let me get a hit on that."

He seemed oblivious to the terse exchange and Owen smiled.

“Oh yeah man, Chloe was just about to, she’s a light weight, then you and me can kill it.” Owen said with a nod and looked to Chloe with a *‘You better fucking do it’* look.

Chloe took the cigarette and took a short puff. Nowhere near as much as she had in the car, but the effects were no less swift in rolling on.

Owen smiled and patted her leg under the table. He leaned in with Declan to share the cigarette, talking quietly between themselves. Chloe tried to listen in at first, but it all just became part of the buzz in the room, punctuated in near perfect time as the band started to play.

Through the cloud of Shift supplanting her thoughts, she could make out the first movement of Beethoven’s Sixth Symphony, affectionately called the

'Pastoral Symphony'. The uptick and down beats of the song seemed to bring to life a choreography to the scene that had been present but was now impossible to miss. The haze and burn behind her eyes started to return. That feeling of stepping out of herself, The Shift, was on her. Though her stomach was turned in on itself, she could feel the tension in her back and shoulders ease as she slid down in the chair, watching herself watch the room.

The Host was saying something, having returned to the stage, but Chloe couldn't piece the words together. She was lost in the daze of her high. Even as the surgeon started to cut into Kammy's hip with the scalpel. Even as the blood started to run down into the crease of her groin, then down her thigh, her knee, and began to drip off her toes. Chloe had thought about being a nurse when she was younger and imagined herself there on the stage with the doctor, checking vitals, placing clamps and gauze, checking catheters, and adjusting medications. She could see it all so clearly, like it was directly in her face.

The chirp and cadence of the first movement of music lent itself eerily well to the activity on stage. It was boisterous and rolling at parts, slow and curious at others, and the surgeon worked his scalpel like a conductor worked a baton. Even as the second movement started, far more somber than the first, it still framed the motions of the scene perfectly.

She underestimated how much fat there would be on a woman as athletically built as Kammy. The doctor sliced and cut with the small scalpel, carving the gluteus medius away in one solid mass. The light blue and yellow tinges of glistening fatty tissue and tendon soon gave way to rich pink meat. His blade continued up and through the anterior hip muscle as he carved, severing the iliopsoas and exposing the upper portion of the femur.

The surgery nurse knelt along Kammy's leg and used one of the stirrups of the medical bed to lift Kammy's leg by the ankle. The nurse did her best to keep Kammy's vulva from being exposed, but the crowd was not above a few cat calls when they got a brief glimpse of her most intimate parts. Apparently Kammy kept a close shave, or simply had been diligent in preparing for the procedure.

"Hey Doc, slice me off a little sliver of that snatch! I'll pay you a million dollars!" Someone called, and was answered with a laugh from the crowd.

"'ll give you two!" Declan yelled to the stage.

He laughed, but Chloe could tell the man wouldn't hesitate to pay two million dollars to suck down a bloody chunk of Kammy's shaved pussy. Chloe's lip curled, and Amada rolled her eyes.

The surgeon was undaunted. He bent down to mark his next cut, making sure to avoid her genitalia entirely. Once the route was mapped, he started with the scalpel again, slipping it into the soft, perfect skin of her inner thigh and making small cuts until the edges of the incision met up with the ones he had started up higher. He continued his way south, cutting a wide berth around her anus as the nurses worked diligently to staunch blood flow with cauterizing rods, and clamping the femoral artery once it became exposed. There was a lot of blood. More than Chloe had ever seen in her life, and though Kammy's vitals dipped marginally, she was stable.

Once he finished making the deep, circuitous cut, the surgeon used clamps and a stainless steel spreader to open the incision wide. Everyone could see the pure white femur, wet and glossy in the overhead lights. He took up his bone saw and he went right to work sawing her femur away from the femoral head, which he left in her hip socket. Chloe grit her teeth, able to feel the vibrations of the steel teeth gnawing into the bone. Even through the rising swell of the symphony's second movement, the vibrations found their way to her. The steady grind of the saw moving back and forth ran up and down her spine. She pressed a fingers to her ears and closed her eyes until the grinding stopped.

There was a small cheer from the crowd and when she opened her eyes, the surgeon was there, holding the entirety of Kammy's perfect leg up for all to see. The end was packed with gauze to keep blood from dripping onto the floor any further. The nurses were all busy around Kammy, stitching and padding and refreshing fluid in bags, a general buzz of activity.

The doctor knelt and offered the leg out to Nando, who accepted it with a small bow and turned. He admired the flesh for a moment, inspecting and making a show of doing so. Finding it to his satisfaction, all semblance of grace or respect was gone as he let the leg drop onto a large red cutting board. The wet slam of dead meat hitting the table startled her.

Nando sharpened his cleaver and went to work chopping. Two chops and off came the foot. Nando used the cleaver to push it aside, and one of his staff scooped it up.

"Sausage." Nando instructed the cook to his left

The man bowed and moved off to a far table and started chopping off toes and piecing the rest of it into smaller chunks to feed into an electric meat grinder that was already buzzing and hungry. The cooks busied themselves with herbs and spices while the meat they stripped from the bone was all ground down into a consistent pink paste.

Nando slid the rest of the leg down his table. Three chops this time, just below the knee and the calf came away. Nando took up a small fillet knife and, much like the surgeon, sliced expertly along the length, and started cutting that flawless skin away from the meat. It was lean, perfectly pink. The skin he tossed aside to the cook who was making sausage, apparently nothing was going to waste. Chloe found that oddly mollifying.

Using the filet knife, Nando cut down the length of the calf muscle, laying the meat out flat like the wings of the butterfly. He sliced it away from the bone and trimmed off the tight tendon that attached it to the shin. Nando worked fast but effectively. Where the surgeon was like a mechanic working on a car, Nando was an artist before a canvas. His knife moved like a calligraphy pen with clean and elegant movements. His blade barely scraped the cutting board as it slid effortlessly through layers of skin and meat. Everything he trimmed and sliced away was scraped aside and picked up by the cook that was taking the spare bits and feeding them into the electric grinder. The little machine was effortlessly turning it all, tendon, fat, skin and everything else, into an evenly textured and colored paste.

When he was done he, had two steaks. Each one he laid out flat, salted, peppered, and hammered with a steel tenderizer. He laid them out on a steel baking sheet and slid them down the table to another cook opposite the one making sausage.

"Rolled flank steak." He said, and moved on.

The cook nodded, took the tray and moved to their station and started chopping vegetables. Bell peppers, onions, mushrooms, and many others that Chloe couldn't see.

Now, Nando moved on to the main course. That succulent thigh and flank laying before him. It was strange, seeing it all being parceled out and prepared. Chloe wasn't thinking of it as a part, or parts, of a human being anymore, it was all just *meat*. She found herself wondering how much that thigh weighed. How much a pound of 'Kammy Roast' would go for at market? She giggled slightly, though she cut it off as the reality came back to her and she turned her eyes back up to the main stage.

Kammy was still there, the rest of her hip joint was removed from her pelvis with a tool that looked similar to an ice cream scoop. The sound Chloe heard as it came free was like someone biting into a crisp apple. She shuddered once more and pressed a finger to her ear reflexively.

Once it was free and the surgeon gave his approval, the nurses began the task of getting her stitched up and cleaned meticulously. Her IV bags were changed and a layer of biological medical foam was applied to the wound before clean bandages were applied. She moaned lightly as she started to wake into the twilight haze of the anesthesia wearing off. Chloe's heart sank and she prayed they kept her doped up enough that she wouldn't realize what exactly was going on. The thought of Kammy waking up to see Nando filleting her own leg would be too much to bear. Chloe took a deep breath and let her mind wander away from the image, though her eyes settled once more on the hunk of meat there on the cutting board.

She marveled once more at just how much fat there was. It was a deep yellow on the surface that gave way to a shade of white that looked almost blue or purple. Each slice of the knife revealing another layer, another shade, that is until that clean and unmistakably pink meat emerged.

Nando cleaned the haunch of meat, like some sort of grizzly fruit emerging from a pulpy rind. The flesh and fat and trimmings went into the grinder. Chloe actually felt a bit of remorse at seeing that pristine shank of skin getting churned down into sausage.

She wasn't a lesbian, but she had a strong and strange desire to run her tongue over it, to taste the skin and sweat of the pop diva. Before she could contemplate it too long, it was fed into the grinder and reduced to that same paste that the cook was kneading and massaging a myriad of spices into.

With a few more expert strokes, Nando had a perfect roast and he wasted no time going to work on it. He started rubbing it down with spices and a dark red sauce he had premixed. He took a fat meat injector and was filling it with that same special sauce. He plunged the bulb head of the syringe deep into the meat and slowly injected it. He withdrew the syringe and repeated it several times on all sides.

The third movement of the music came to its marching crescendo and then the high call of the oboe soothed the tune to its more furtive conclusion before the fourth movement began, sounding more grim and ominous than the previous fun frolicking tones of the prior movements.

“Normally. The meat would marinate and rest for twenty four hours, then be braised for eight to twelve hours. Obviously we don’t have that sort of time, and I think you all want it fresh anyway, hm?” Nando said as he skewered the roast straight up through the femur dramatically.

“Instead, our gracious host has provided us a state of the art, infrared ceramic roasting oven.” Nando said as one of his assistants brought a wheeled table around with a white and silver contraption that looked more like a satellite dish than an oven. Nando up-ended the roast and plugged the spit straight down into the center of the dish, standing it up right where it started to rotate slowly.

It reminded Chloe of the porcelain ballerina in her jewelry box she had when she was young, though much more clumsy and dripping with oil,spices, and blood. With the flick of a switch, the edges of the dish started to glow a radiant orange, and the sizzle of meat and pop of cooking fat could be heard almost immediately after.

At the side tables, the steaks from Kammy's calf were laid out, lined with vegetables and a bread dressing and then rolled into tight coils and skewered to hold their positions. Each of these round "loaves" was then placed into a skillet that was bubbling with a layer of butter and what smelled like garlic.

On the opposite table, the sausages were being stuffed into casings and then similarly fried. The fifth and final movement of the music started with a gentle and lively flare; it was accompanied by the static hissof sizzling meats. Nando moved from station to station, peppering or salting, testing and prodding.

Meanwhile, the cooks moved about, cleaning up and starting to prepare plates and silverware. Chloe was aware that her champagne flute had been refilled, but she wasn't sure when it had happened. The smells in the air; butter, garlic, savory meat, and frying vegetables all mingled and hit her nose, causing a gush of saliva to invade her mouth. She had been so enthralled in watching the meal preparation that she hardly noticed how close Declan and Owen were and how animated their conversation was.

It was completely lost on her to that point. Amada just still looked unpleasantly bored. All around them, people were engaged in conversation; laughing and sipping their champagne, talking business in low tones, or outright sharing jokes at Kammy's expense.

One older man, whom Chloe thought she recognized, rose and moved to the stage, speaking quietly to the doctor. He was given a nod and he stepped up onto the stage, leaving a long and overly wet kiss on Kammy's drug-addled cheek.

The girl whimpered gently and tried to open her eyes. The man gave a discreet grope of her breast and moved off the stage. A mild round of amused applause went up in his wake. Chloe recognized the man then, as he smiled while offering a small, humble bow. She had seen him on the news too: Archdiocese Milton Lane. He had been tried and exonerated of molesting the kids in his church a few years back. With friends like he had in this room, it was no wonder he got off the hook. Chloe felt gross all over, her heart aching for Kammy yet again.

Chloe ignored some of the looks she was getting and she wished she hadn't worn something so revealing. She would have killed for a big parka right then. She was shrinking into herself and thinking about going to the coat check when Amada stood up suddenly.

"I have to use the bathroom. Chloe, come with me." She said, not asking, but commanding.

"Oh… okay." Chloe said. Not really having to use it but she agreed anyway.

"You girls have fun." Declan said with a sleazy grin.

Amada lead them up the row of tables in the direction they had entered, then along the velveteen wall and past the gallery of framed artworks. Most of the paintings were Rembrandt-esque portraits of older men and women. The expressions on their faces were all the same taciturn mask of disapproval. Chloe shivered and lowered her gaze to the floor, she could feel the eyes following her as she passed. She hurried to keep pace with Amada.

As they neared the bathrooms, two older women were coming out, both of them in furs and pearls like they were out for a night at the opera. They smiled curtly to Chloe as Amada blew right past them.

The walls within the bathroom were that same deep red, but with a golden floral brocade that extended from floor to ceiling. The bathroom was old and rustic, like something from a Victorian play, complete with clawfoot sinks and powder jars on the counters. There was a long bronze framed mirror that extended the length of the wall above the sinks. Amada immediately went to one the stalls and shut the door, Chloe did the same, choosing the one adjacent.

Fortunately, the music from outside was piped in, allowing her to forget that she could clearly hear Amada next to her and she could likely be heard in kind. Luckily, Chloe wasn't shy. Amada finished first and when Chloe stepped out of the stall, she could see the Slavic woman stooped over a pile of white powder on the edge of the sink. Amada made a neat little row of lines with a black credit card and leaned down, inhaling one into her left nostril and one into her right.

"Cocaine?" Amada offered as Chloe came out.

"You sure that's a good idea?" Chloe asked, motioning the open bathroom around them.

"We are about to watch a human being be eaten on international waters. A little blow is the least of anyone's concern." She replied casually snorting back once, then twice.

"Fair enough, but no, thanks. I used to have a real problem with it." Chloe said, her mouth watering at the sight of her drug of choice and, her palms began sweating at the refusal.

"Too bad. It's good. It will keep your appetite down." Amada said and inhaled the last two lines as well.

She dusted the edge of the sink off and looked herself over in the mirror. She dabbed at her eyes and reapplied her makeup, watching Chloe in the reflection.

"Looks like it… thanks for offering though." Chloe said, moving to a sink to freshen up as well.

"You know if you mention anything about this night…" Amada started, meeting Chloe's eyes in the mirror.

"No no, I can imagine, I think I saw the state prosecutor sitting with a former vice president out there. I'd probably end up so far gone I might as well have never existed." Chloe said, a small shiver going through her. This caused Amada a genuine smile.

"Smart girl. You sure you are ready for what comes next?" Amada asked, all the threats she had lined up melting off as she closed up her purse and started out.

“Ready as I’ll ever be I guess.” Chloe chewed her lip feeling like she had just escaped a tiger den and followed Amada back to the table.

“You’re just in time.” Owen said as they arrived. “They’re serving plates.”

The smell in the dining room was divine. The myriad of savory smells were heavy in the air. She could hear the crackling of fatty meat as it turned slowly on the spit, the fat caramelizing and the meat browning under the intense heat of the convection spit it was roasting on. As it turned, Nando was slicing and shaving slivers off onto a serving plate. Each piece falling away with hardly a tease of the knife.

The wait staff was in full swing now, preparing plates. The sausages had been pan fried and diced into medallions, which were then placed vertically into the cap of a stuffed mushroom. Each plate got three of them onto a side.

Next was the rolled steaks made from Kammy's calves. Each tenderized and stuffed roll was then sliced. The shape of it reminded Chloe of a cinnamon roll, except it was meat and bell peppers instead of a flaky pastry. Each plate had a rolled steak lovingly laid onto it before it made its way to the main course station.

As Nando sliced meat from the haunch that spun and cooked before him, the shavings were then laid into fresh corn tortillas, topped with what appeared to be a pico de gallo salsa, and decorated with cilantro and some spinach shavings. Chloe hated how hungry she was right then. She hated how good it smelled. She hated how badly she wanted to eat it.

By the time her black ceramic plate was laid before her along with a fresh glass of champagne, her untouched glass having been removed. Most of the others in the dining hall were served and already eating without ceremony. Declan and Owen dug right in, their eyes rolling back at the sensation and flavor that hit them. Amada picked at hers, but clearly the cocaine was doing its job. Chloe hesitated, and picked up one of the mushrooms and popped it, sausage medallion and all, into her mouth.

Her palate exploded to life with flavor and she started in to her meal with a hunger that bordered on passion, her enjoyment bordering on orgasmic. It was a genuine synaptic storm in her brain as the flavor receptors in her mouth fired in ways they never had before. She could feel herself blushing, her nipples getting hard, her panties getting wet. She sliced and diced and skewered, and had to pace herself to keep from shoving it all greedily into her mouth like Declan and Owen were doing.

In fact, everyone seemed to be eating with a reptilian hunger that caused them to eschew manners and protocol, even in such refined company. Men had grease running down into the sleeves of their expensive suits. People dropped their forks and knives and scooped up meat with their hands, sucking every bit of flavor from their knuckles. One woman had a line of grease that ran down her chin and into the V-neck of her top. The men adjacent to her on either side were taking turns lapping it up from her cleavage. At their own table, Amada was stroking Declan's cock through his pants under the table as he grunted and slobbered over his plate. She felt Owen's leg ram against hers under the table and she pressed hers right back against his. She thought about climbing onto the table and letting him fuck her right there, but then, she would have to stop eating, and that wasn't going to happen.

It was a feeding frenzy. The noises around her were a cascade of inhuman grunts and wet squelches. It was so loud it nearly drowned out the music. Chloe could only barely make out the fifth and final movement of the symphony. The rest of the room sounded like a feasting scene from some B-grade zombie movie and looked painfully similar.

On the stage, Kammy was still in the twilight of her anesthesia, though Chloe could see her eyes cracked open and looking around. It almost made her sick, though she couldn't bring herself to slow her eating. That was until the Host came out onto the stage, a broad smile on his face, his hands wringing in smug satisfaction. There was an unmistakable flash across

Chloe's field of vision and for a split second, the host was transformed.

He was no longer the aged gentleman in the pressed suit. He was now naked, and standing nearly seven feet tall. His skin was red and mottled with black streaks of pigment. His feet had become cloven hooves, and his knees seemed to have reversed. In that vision, he had revealed himself to be The Devil, and they were all his demons: Writhing, grease-soaked and bloody. Around them the room became a vision of Hell itself.

The walls dripped with congealed fat and the floor was pooled with thick black oil. Huge veins pulsed through the seams of the floor and walls, like black tree roots, creating pools of fleshy naked bodies all feasting and fucking on one another.

Their fluids splashed about as they ate until they regurgitated and re-consumed. All of them taking turns spooning matter from the same holes they defecated and forcing it into their gaping mouths. They groped blindly, lewdly, and slithered across one another, thrusting engorged flesh into any orifice they could find. The music had dropped in pitch by several octaves and droned horrifically in her ears.

She could feel the table under her had grown spongy and wet. The furniture all around her was writhing along with the bodies around them, creating an indiscernible, undulating, organic mass. Owen, Declan, and Amada lurched into and against one another like maggots fighting on the back of a rotten pig. She felt something hard and wet wrap around her leg and she opened her mouth to scream, only to feel the mass of her tongue lurch free of her mouth like a groping tentacle.

Chloe flinched away from the table, hard. She nearly threw herself back onto the floor, only to realize it had all vanished, and everything was back to normal. The music had stopped. Her plate was empty, the spell was broken and she was there, sweaty, disheveled, and full to the brim.

She could see others around her coming out of the trance, though several of them seemed to be able to laugh it off, others seemed slightly troubled, as she did. Others were still caught up in the throes of passion and were grunting out ejaculations manually or bouncing their dates in their laps, skirts hiked up about their waists. No one seemed to care.

"Come on Kammy." The Host piped up suddenly overhead through the speakers. "Look at all these adoring fans. Why not sing them a little something, hm? Show them your appreciation."

How could he even ask that of her? Chloe felt ashamed at the frenzy that had taken place, and that she had been a part of it. Now to ask her to sing? It was almost too much, but once Kammy started up, Chloe stopped fretting and looked up to the stage, her eyes getting wet with tears.

"Some.... Where... over the rainbow..." Kammy started, sounding tired, her throat hoarse, but her voice was clear enough and sweet. The Host gave her a sip of water from the steel cup once more, and she went on. The room fell silent as Kammy's voice lilted through the speakers overhead. Chloe's heart fluttered and swelled as the song came to her. The sleepy, somber tone in Kammy's voice nearly broke her heart.

"Way up hiiigh

"There's a land that I've heard of once in a lullaby

Somewhere over the rainbow, skies are blue.

And dreams that you dare to dream

Really do come true...."

It was then Kammy faltered. A single tear rolling down her cheek and her voice hitched as she struggled to find the words, though they failed to come to her.

The room started to buzz again, the spell of her song almost breaking. Chloe took a deep breath and rose, continuing the song. Her voice was clearer, stronger, and just as sweet.

"Someday I'll wish upon a star...

And wake up where the clouds are far behind meeee...

Where troubles melt like lemon drops,

Way up above the chimney tops,

That's where you'll find me."

Kammy smiled brightly, some of the color returning to her cheeks as her eyes searched the room for Chloe. Chloe moved out into the aisle, approaching the stage. Every eye in the room, including Kammy's, was on her as both of the women continued in the perfect melody of a duet.

"Somewhere over the rainbow, blue birds fly

Birds fly over the rainbow,

Why then, oh why can't I

If happy little bluebirds fly beyond the rainbow

Why, oh why can't I?"

Their voices lingered long in the acoustics of the hall and fell on a perfect silence as Chloe and Kammy met eyes there in the dim light. Kammy looked serene and peaceful. She nodded once and laid her head back, falling into sleep.

Chloe was suddenly aware that everyone was still looking at her and she turned, blushing hotly. The blush intensified as the room broke out into a standing ovation. She waved and offered an awkward curtsy before she headed back to the table offering small waves and bright smiles to all she passed.

Owen was clapping too, having cleaned up, best as he was able, after the feast.

“Holy shit ‘Lo, I haven’t heard you sing that one since what? High school?”

“Yeah well, what can I say?” She said sheepishly, missing the use of the hated nickname.

Owen leaned over to Declan. "She sang that at a talent show in school, not a dry eye in the house. Got her a choir scholarship for it too."

Declan was visibly impressed.

"Hey you guys rode the raft out right? Fuck that, I want you to fly back with me on my chopper. Cool?"

Owen looked to Chloe, who nodded, anything to keep from having to get on that inflatable boat in the cold again.

"Cool." Owen confirmed.

As the small helicopter took off from the flight deck of the ship, the rain was just starting to come down. Chloe didn't have an ounce of sympathy for those that had to get onto the open air motor boat for the hour plus trip back. She watched the lights of the ship fall away from them and disappear into the black swirl of ocean beneath.

"So Chloe. Owen tells me you're looking to kick your career up a few notches. I think I can help with that. If you're interested." Declan said, lighting a cigarette and leaning towards her, as much as the harness of his seat would allow.

It was loud in the small helicopter, and Declan had to yell over the whir of the blades. The look of shock and mild disgust must have been evident on her face..

"Don't get too excited now." He laughed.

"No no. I just… I wasn't expecting it and I don't know. After what I saw tonight?" Chloe said with a small shake of her head.

“What about it? Oh I get it, you think that thing with Kammy was what? A punishment? No no, Kid, what you saw was a deification. We just spent the last few hours worshiping that woman.”

“Oh is *that* what that was?” Chloe asked, venom in her voice.

Owen tried to put an arm around her and she shrugged him off. “We fucking ate part of that poor girl, what about her leg? She’s… she’s disfigured now.”

“Sure, but next week, when the news report comes out about a tragic accident involving poor beloved Kammy Luv? Imagine the outcry of support. The comeback she’ll have if her people play it right. Sympathy sells!”

Chloe shook her head, but Declan went on, his cigarette in hand punctuating his speech. She could see now where Owen had picked up the gesticulation.

"Look, Kammy has been on her way out for years now. She's been riding the success of a song she wrote when she was sixteen for almost a decade. She's a fading star and she knows it. She can keep trying to pump out generic dance hall tunes until she's too old to appeal to the thirteen to twenty-one year olds. Or…" He trailed off, taking a long drag of his cigarette.

"Or she can have an… 'accident' and grow up, mature, and start a new demographic." Owen chipped in.

This earned him a nod and a point from Declan.

"Exactly. She becomes a survivor, a symbol of strength. A role model. Most pop stars have to come off drugs or be abused by a spouse, or some rock-bottom shit like that. Kammy though? She gets to do it on her own terms. Not to mention, did Owen tell you how much each plate at this soiree sold for?" He asked, looking to Owen who shook his head.

Chloe looked between them, curiosity on her face.

"One. Million. Dollars. Kammy Luv made over thirty million as part of her take alone tonight. Yeah Owen here owes me a pretty penny, but, you might turn out to be worth it." Declan grinned. "If you decide to talk to my people."

“Wait. A million? Dollars? Each!? Owen you don’t have that!” Chloe looked to him, Owen looked a little sheepish.

“Yeah Declan sort of… fronted me… if I brought you along.” Owen admitted.

“He promised fresh meat. If you’ll pardon the pun. And Kid, you delivered tonight. That impromptu duet? You should have seen the big wigs popping wood over you.” Declan said, trying to sound supportive, but as seemed to be his usual, sounded totally sleazy.

Chloe sat back against the seat. She wanted to be mad at Owen. She felt used, and more than a little betrayed. She was no fool though, and had been in the business long enough to know that was how it got played. She wanted to be mad at Owen, but she wasn’t, she couldn’t be.

"Look. We all get devoured in this business Kid. You can choose who eats how much, or you can let it swallow you whole. You play your cards right, you'll be in a position to be on the stage at an event like this after years of a successful career. Or… you can keep doing car commercial jingles until you cave and do some porn flicks for some grease-ball in a hotel room. Either way, someone is going to get a piece. And I'm sure you know it can be really ugly when it happens. You though? You can decide where and when." Declan sat back, for the first time, Chloe noticed Amada was smiling to her, warmly this time.

"Alright." Chloe said after a long moment. "Have your people call my people. Let's do lunch."

Artist Credit

"*Little Stevie*" – By Colter Burkey

Colter Burkey was born in Scottsbluff, Nebraska where his artistic endeavors began early in childhood. He continued to pursue art at Midland University, earning his BA in Fine Art and Graphic Design. It was during this time that Colter won the Mercedes Augustine Award for success and talent both in the studio and classroom.

Currently, He keeps himself occupied with commissions ranging from tattoo designs to logos. His online works can be found on

Instagram: @weepinggrimm

Facebook: facebook.com/AskASatanist.

-

"*Bloody Footprints*" – By Dave Lipscomb

A native of Providence, R.I., Dave Lipscomb began creating art at the age of onc. Years later, he enrolled in Paier College of Art, INC. and earned a B.F.A. in Illustration. Various freelance work soon followed, including painted tapestries, portraits, and airbrush designs on clothing.

A current resident of Southern California since the early 90s, other accomplishments have included his work appearing in the indy comic books POVERTY PACK, POVERTY THRILL ADVENTURES, and most recently the epic historically-based fantasy adventure series THE MAROON. From April 2012 to April 2016, he was the illustrator and music columnist for INFERNAL INK MAGAZINE: DEVILISHLY EROTIC HORROR. Other noteworthy publications include the similarly-themed essay anthology BELIALIAN WOMAN: THE COMPLETE COLLECTION, the cover of author Rick Powell's debut benefit poetry collection MY SOUL STAINED, MY SEED SOUR, the cover of V.Z. LaValle's anthology CRACKS IN THE WALLS, and THE HORROR AND MADNESS OF THE SIDESHOW, featuring written works from members of the audio drama troupe The Satanic Players Society.

Generous samples of Dave's work can be seen on his Facebook page The DaveL's Gallery and on Instagram, where he goes by the handle the_dave_l. Many of the illustrations from some of the aforementioned publications can be seen as well as his raw, yet highly detailed sketchbook entries.

-

“*Vacant Eyes*” – By Joel Greaves

Joel Greaves aka GBH Tattooist/mixed media artist based in the gold coast of Queensland Australia. Influenced by a wide range of art styles including tattoo art, horror, classic, comic and fantasy.

Check out his art Instagram: gbhtat2

Photography Instagram: joel_greaves_666

Or contact him at: joeltat2@y7mail.com

-

“*Kammy Luv*” – By Sylvia de Vries – Ribbers

“*Cannibalia*” – By Sylvia de Vries – Ribbers

Sylvia de Vries – Ribbers is a Dutch surreal contemporary artist, specialised in horror and the bizarre. She takes her inspiration from the human anatomy, (dark) folk and fairy tales and the darkness of the mind.

Ever since she could hold a pencil, she has been drawing and colouring. Fairy tales and Disney have been her first inspiration, but ever since she was little there was still that part of her that liked the dark and unusual. Now she tries to combine those two styles into one, showing people the most scary thing on earth is what is in the peoples own minds.

Besides her own work as form of Art Therapy, she does various submissions from portraits of loved ones and animals to tattoo designs and book illustrations.

She is also an artist at Gift Horse Productions, an art team situated in the Washington state of the USA. Examples of her work can be found on her Facebook page, Instagram and website.

Made in the USA
Coppell, TX
03 July 2020

About the Author

William Tull is an independent American author whose previous works include short stories published in *"Infernal Ink Magazine: Devilishly Erotic Horror"* and screenplays for various horror themed podcasts and audio dramas. He and his family operate a small dairy farm, which keeps him busy when he is not attempting to conjure tales of mystery and madness. He enjoys spending his time both in front of the camera, and behind it with the crew of Toonsmith Studios; an independent film studio in the Pacific Northwest.

Comments, questions, and all feedback are welcome, and he encourages you to reach out to him at his personal email: hornsandhooves@yahoo.com.